FORM AND FURY

THE MISTS OF ELISTA TRILOGY, BOOK 3

CLARA WILS

Gryphon's Gate Publishing

Form and Fury

Copyright © 2022 Clara Wils

Gryphon's Gate Publishing

550 King St. N.

PO Box 42088 Conestoga

Waterloo, ON

N2L 6K5

ISBN: 978-1-990587-01-6

Print ISBN: 978-1-990587-02-3

CHAPTER 1

Prince Alvere of Vauphan and I stood atop a newly constructed watch tower, his arm around my shoulder. I leaned into him, sliding my arm around his waist. We could see the distant ramparts of the Elistan camp. Closer to home were the earthwork and palisade the Vauphani were constructing. After the raid on the Vauphan camp twelve days ago, the Vauphani didn't have the numbers for any sort of offensive action. They had to dig in and defend. And the hope was, after this coming night, the Elistans wouldn't be able to form another assault either.

"You should be telling me I'm crazy," I said softly. "Railing against me going out there. Telling me it's futile and that I just want revenge for the death of Maverick."

Alvere shrugged. "Would it do any good?"

"No."

"I didn't think so."

"Am I crazy?" I asked, a hint of uncertainty creeping into my voice.

The plan we'd devised had two parts. First, a small group of us from Maverick House would sneak into the

Elistan Camp — shape-shifted into our small avatars — and take out the Elistan leadership. In particular, I'd vowed to kill Lord War and Lady Claw. The hope was that, without leadership, the Elistans wouldn't be able to mount any sort of assault. The forces here would be stuck in a stalemate. Second, a group of Fey in the Vauphani camp — those whose magic pertained to metal — were already performing a lengthy ritual. When they unleashed their power at dawn tomorrow, it would hex most, if not all, of the metal in the Elistan camp. Armor would burn when worn, weapons would sear the hands that held them. Between our attack and the curse, we hoped that would keep the Elistan forces at bay.

After that, House Maverick — no we were House Spider now — would return to our nation, to cut out the rot of corruption within Elista. I had no clue how we were going to do that... but one step at a time.

"You'd have to be crazy to do what you're planning," Alvere whispered, "but I've accepted it. Crazy or not, I love you." He turned to kiss me on the cheek. I shifted so I could meet his lips in a quick, chaste kiss. I knew he was a prince — technically a king now — and who he married would be out of his hands. It certainly wouldn't be me. But we'd have some time together before that happened, maybe even after, depending on how possessive his future wife was. I was certainly willing to share.

And that thought made me think of Silence and Sparrow, my other lovers. I longed for them as much as I ached to be with Alvere. I hadn't been with any of them these last few nights as we'd planned our counter-attack upon Panther House and its forces. But I'd seen Alvere and Silence and Sparrow together from time to time. Given Silence had had some reservations about the prince, I asked Alvere, "Has Silence spoken to you... about... us?"

He nodded. "Yes." Alvere smiled. "While you were laid up Silence and I had a long talk. Silence even... kissed me." He touched his lips. Alvere seemed confused yet pleasantly surprised.

I raised a brow. That was a turn-around indeed.

"I had a chance to speak a little with Sparrow as she healed as well. They are wonderful and kind people and I see how much they love you," Alvere continued. "We may come from different places and different backgrounds but we all agree on one thing: our love for you." He sighed; voice tinged with shame when he said, "Despite the atrocities my people committed upon him, Silence seems to have forgiven me. I... I don't know how or why. He is truly a kind and generous soul."

"That he is. I'm glad you two are getting along. I'm very much looking forward to being with... both of you."

Alvere raised a brow and the curious intensity in his jewel-blue eyes let me know what he thought of that idea.

But that wouldn't happen tonight. Tonight would be for a different kind of action and excitement. Yet once this mission was done and we could take a well-needed break from things, I planned on getting all three of them together and *celebrating*.

I might even see if Ant wished to join our strange group of communal love. The large man was still devastated by Amber's death. It was clear, he loved her, even if he'd never admitted his love. She'd known, we all knew it, but I could see now how much it weighed on Ant that he'd never fully expressed himself to her. I vowed not to make that same mistake. Those I loved would know it.

And those I loved now included an entire Noble House.

I was in charge and would need to care for all of them. It may have been a small house, so few members now, but that made it all the easier to know each one of them deeply. I didn't know half of them as well as I should, something else I vowed to change.

They had come together to help me escape the devastating dread and depression I'd fallen into after the death of Maverick, Amber, Jack, Tusk and Fennec. I still blamed myself for their deaths, just a little. But I also blamed the Elistan Nobles who'd actually killed them. And in the end, I knew they'd gone into that fight willingly, knowing they might need to lay down their lives for myself, for their House, and for peace between these two nations.

It was such an odd concept that for peace, some people had to die. I had hoped that wouldn't be the case, I had tried to talk to the Elistans — my own people — to get them to stop this madness, but to no avail. Those who led this army were part of a shadowy group of Nobles. They were the true enemy. They'd started this war, though we still didn't know why, and they'd also been killing off any Nobles — and their True-Bonded Lumani — who opposed them.

Tonight, I'd stop this war before those vicious Nobles could do more damage. The warmonger: Lord War, Field Marshal of the Elistan armies, would die so he couldn't retaliate. And Lady Claw would die for killing Maverick, that I had vowed. I hoped those who died tonight would be the last of this war... but I feared they wouldn't be.

The sun began to set.

"I need to get to my people and organize them," I said breaking away from Alvere.

"There's something I'd like to show you first, a bit of a surprise, if you'll allow it."

"What is it?"

"A surprise," he said with a mischievous grin. "Come on, I'll show you."

Curious, I followed him down the ladder of the watch tower. He walked fast, knowing I was needed elsewhere. I kept pace easily, as tall as him but with a bit more leg on me. His black hair shimmered with raven-blue highlights in the evening's dim light; his brilliant jewel-blue eyes dancing with life. I'd learned that these — along with his pale skin — were traits of the Fey. They were small and pale with dark hair and jewel-tone eyes. Alvere was half-Fey, but that was not widely known.

"Where are we going?" I asked, curiosity growing as we passed farther and farther to the back of our camp.

"You'll see." He grinned and winked at me. "Here," he said a moment later as we came around some tents to the makeshift smithy that had been set up by one of the Fey. I hadn't seen it done, but people said stones had been summoned from the earth to form the large forge-hearth and chimney, then a tent had been put up around it.

When we entered no one was there, and the forge was cold. The Fey smith who worked here would be helping the others who had affinity with metal perform the ritual to curse Elistan weapons and armor.

Alvere went to a long table on one side of the tent and picked up something before turning to me.

"What do you think?" he asked, holding up a beautiful breastplate. "I had Eorthan make a whole set of armor for you."

I moved in and ran my hands over the odd-looking metal. If it was steel, it had a strange golden burnish to it. "What is it made from?" I asked in awe, feeling the smooth curves of the armor. He handed it over to me and it felt light as air.

"It's steel, but Fey-forged, with their own unique magic." He grinned wildly. "Go ahead, put it on."

"There are no straps," I said, looking at the formed metal. "How do I put it on?"

He smiled and took the breastplate from me, then simply held it to my front. I felt an odd sensation, as if it was sucking itself against me, molding to my form. When Alvere released it, the armor stayed in place perfectly. What was more... it seemed to move with me, bend and flex as if it were cloth.

"Amazing," I breathed in awe. "I could get used to this." I looked up at him with excitement. "You said there was more?"

He helped me into the full suit: a breastplate and back-plate, pauldrons and coverings for the upper arm, then bracers. A solid metal "skirt" in two halves, which fused together when put on the front and back of me, then it relaxed and moved like silk, even though it was hard as steel. Finally, there were grieves and even a pair of metal boots, which fit better than any leather set I'd ever had, comfortable and snug.

"This is incredible!" I gushed.

Have you seen anything like this before? I asked Auwei, the Lumani spirit who dwelled within me.

No, it's so light and comfortable. I've only worn armor for a couple of my previous lives and never much liked the feel of it, but this... this is a miracle!

And it was, truly.

"Thank you!" I said, overwhelmed with gratitude, throwing my arms around Alvere in a tight embrace.

"Thank Eorthan," Alvere said. "He's the one who made it. I'll introduce you tomorrow, once he's done with his ritual and you're... safely back here with me."

"I will," I said, growing solemn again, releasing him from the embrace to look him in the eye. Time was short, and I'd soon be away. I knew he was concerned for me. He'd given me this gift to protect me. "And I will return safely as well. I promise."

He nodded, but I could see the worry in his beryl-blue eyes.

As we made our way back to his pavilion he said: "There is another surprise I have waiting for you."

I was curious but patient. The first surprise had been amazing, so I hoped the next was just as good.

When we entered his pavilion five Fey in black cloaks stood off to one side. Also present were those going on the mission tonight: Midnight, Ant, Foggy, and Sparrow. The rest of my House: Fin, Princess, Dove, and Silence would be staying behind, but they were all here for this final briefing.

"Before you begin," Alvere said, raising his voice so all could hear, "I wish to aid you in tonight's mission. So, I have arranged for a few Fey to accompany you." He raised a hand at my stunned look and the questions he knew must be coming. "Surprise," he said with a just-try-and-stop-me grin. Then, "They have their own way of moving unseen and unhindered by walls and obstructions." He nodded to the group.

One of them stepped forward. Their cloak began to flap about them and they lifted from the ground slowly. At the same time, they seemed to fade into the darkness at the fringes of the tent. After a moment I had trouble seeing them and had to keep blinking to see their barely-there silhouette. In deeper darkness, they'd have been invisible.

"Thank you," Alvere said and the Fey landed, becoming visible again. That one continued forward, pushing back the hood of their cloak. It was a woman, small and slight with the Fey's pale skin, raven hair, and sharp features.

"I am Ahmaia, and I serve at The Uniter's will." She bowed to Alvere.

"Uniter?" I whispered to Alvere.

"Long story," he said. And now wasn't the time for it. I'd ask him again later.

Ahmaia rose and looked up at me. "We will aid as we can, but we will not kill. Life is most sacred to our kind." Her rose-gold eyes were hard, firm. In their depths I felt a weight of wisdom and age, though she seemed no older than myself. But then, Midnight was half Fey and seemed young, even though she was undoubtedly the oldest member of our — no, *my* — House. I didn't know how old she was, but I got the feeling she was past her fiftieth year at least. Ahmaia seemed older still.

"Understood," I said. "I appreciate your help."

Ahmaia nodded and returned to the other Fey.

I took command from there. "The plan is simple," I said, looking at each of my people in turn. Alvere leaned against a support post for the tent and smiled, watching me be all boss-like.

"Midnight will go in just after full dark and scout the locations of the leaders in the camp." I turned to Ahmaia. "Is that something you or one of yours could do as well?"

She nodded. "We will all go, that will expedite things, yes?"

"Yes, very much so. Just be back before the moon is at its zenith. That's when we'll regroup and set out. If the leaders are all close, we'll go as one team, if they're not, we'll divide up as needed. Our three primary targets are Lord War, Lady Claw, and Lord Jaguar."

"Jaguar's mine," Ant growled and the raw hatred and vehemence in the usually jovial man's voice made me flinch.

"Understood. Lady Claw is mine," I said, hopefully a bit less frighteningly. "Our secondary targets are any other high-ranking members of Panther House who would be able to take charge of their forces in the absence of the others. We want to leave no potential leaders alive."

"Might they be captured?" Ahmaia asked.

"We have no way of bringing them back here," I said.

"We do," the enigmatic Fey woman said with understated efficacy.

"Then yes, capture them and return them here. I'd prefer not to kill if necessary." Which then begged the question: did we *need* to kill War and Claw and Jaguar?

Perhaps not, but I didn't think I could stop Ant... and I wasn't sure I wanted to stop myself from dealing with Claw. I hated her with a fire in my soul which burned night and day and threatened to eat me up if I didn't do something about it.

I guess we'd see how the night went.

"Any questions?"

Foggy, standing on his head, as usual, said, "You already killed the one who killed my brother, didn't you?"

"Yes." Lynx, my old flame from long ago had killed Fennec, Foggy's brother. I'd then killed Lynx when he'd come for me next.

"Then I think we should try to capture as many as we can. We don't know who on their side knows the real reasons for this war. We shouldn't punish them all for something they may not know about."

Fair. "I'm fairly certain War, Claw, and Jaguar know," I said. "But you're right, outside of that we don't know and should not punish them for following orders. Capture if you can, work with the Fey." I turned to Ahmaia. "How many can you capture and bring back?" I assumed the answer was one each, but I'd learned not to underestimate the Fey.

Ahmaia considered for a moment. "Perhaps six or seven each?"

I blinked. "How?"

Ahmaia smiled. "Our cloaks and clothes are enchanted, there are pockets within where we might store... more than usually would be possible."

I didn't bother asking how. It was Fey magic. Giant-super-pockets, sure, I'd accept that. I had a glowing ball of spirit inside of me, granting me powers, so who was I to question strange things.

I am far more than a glowing ball of spirit, Auwei said indignant.

Yes, you are, apologies.

I nodded to the others. "It's nearly sunset. Let's all get something to eat and a bit of rest... Tonight we end this war.

CHAPTER 2

SPARROW CARRIED ANT AND MYSELF. MIDNIGHT AND FOGGY could fly on their own, as could the Fey. I heard the faint fluttering of the fabric of their black cloaks but couldn't see them in the night. One Fey would accompany each of us. Our scouts had told us the leaders were scattered throughout the camp, though there was a concentration of a few near the center of the camp. Perhaps they thought themselves safe there.

They were wrong.

I'd woven a small sail for myself, and when Sparrow let me go, I floated down slowly. Ant wouldn't be coming with me. Jaguar was elsewhere, and he'd promised his revenge on the man.

I was going after Lord War and Lady Claw. It seemed they shared a bed now. It hadn't taken that long after Lynx's death for Claw to move on. I didn't really mind. It made my job that much easier.

I landed lightly and, through my spider-sense, I knew three allies were nearby. One was Midnight, the other two were the Fey accompanying each of us. Still in spider form, I crawled under the tent flap to the dimly lit interior of the large pavilion. There were a few guards within, dicing. When the two Fey moved through the tent-flap, the guards looked but saw nothing of course. A moment later, the four men let out muffled screams as cloth reached out to cover their mouths. I couldn't quite make sense of how the Fey 'pockets' worked, but the four men were swept into the cloaks and simply vanished. The two Fey, one of them being Ahmaia then shimmered to become more visible. I transformed and Midnight stepped out of the shadows. She put a finger to her lips. Not that the signal for quiet was really needed.

She motioned to the central room and held up two fingers and pointed to me. So... War and Claw were in there. And from the grunts and moans escaping through the canvas, I thought I knew what they were doing.

Ahmaia drew close and whispered in my ear. "I sense your desire to kill. Is this truly needed?"

Yes, Legs, is this truly what you want? I sensed Auwei's reservations. One of the reasons the Lumani Bonded with us was to have new and interesting physical experiences of the world. But killing wasn't one that Auwei wished to participate in. She felt my grief as her own. Even though their Lumani would have survived and returned to the Mists, those in my House who'd been killed had been to her as they had been to me, like family. Still, she did not wish for death as a revenge.

For a moment I hesitated. Was death what I wanted?

But then I remembered the hot blood pouring down onto me as Maverick died, the look of mad glee in Claw's eyes as she'd torn out the man's throat.

"The man can live," I whispered back. It might prove useful to have Lord War as a hostage. "The woman dies."

I felt Auwei's sigh of resignation. She didn't like this, didn't approve, but she'd allow me to do what I felt was necessary.

Ahmaia's eyes were hard, gazing at me for a long moment, but she eventually nodded. "I will take the man."

We moved to the tent flap. I veered into my spider to scuttle under the cloth. Ahmaia would know when to enter. She'd told me as much before we'd left.

I tried to ignore the sounds of passion from the bed and scampered along the ground to the far bed leg then up that to peer over the top.

The two were in the throes of passion, the large man kneeling as he drove himself into her. Claw's legs were wide, pushed to the side so he could get in close. He loomed over her, one hand rough on a breast, the other on her throat. Claw gasped and writhed, and somehow still seemed thrilled by this violent sex.

Even though my spider form was small, I didn't want to risk getting any closer than this. Despite their distraction I was sure I'd be noticeable against the pale sheets in the dim light.

So, I simply transformed where I was and stabbed at Claw with my short sword. She had no clue, eyes rolled back in blissful delirium, but War was quick to notice my transformation and lurched them both to one side, such that my blade only nicked Claw's shoulder. War leaped off and away from Claw to land on the other side of the bed. I was just a little distracted by the immensity of his glistening erection, and it was that moment of hesitation which cost me a quick victory.

Claw was up quickly and spun to kick the sword from my hand with a hissed, "Bitch!" My sword went flying. Even as I tried to draw my other, she lunged, claws out. I had to use both hands to block her. One of my hands caught her wrist, the other only adjusted her clawed strike slightly such that instead of it tearing out my neck the claws raked down the side of my face, not deeply, but enough to sting and bleed.

Ahmaia was in the room, I noticed through my periphery, even though I hadn't seen the tent flap move. War turned toward her as lengths of cloth reached out from her. But then he vanished... no, veered.

Claw tried to use her free hand the strike again, but as she reared back, I landed a quick stunning punch to her jaw. I then grasped her neck, squeezing, hoping she hadn't caught enough breath yet and I'd be able to weaken her, but I should have recalled how she'd found such things exciting.

She smiled, eyes flaring with pleasure. Her claws raked over my arm, skidding off my bracer before finding a small, unprotected area on the inside of my elbow. She tore at my flesh and kicked at the same time. I blocked with my own raised leg. I wouldn't be able to maintain my grip on her neck with my forearm torn open, so I simply threw her to the ground with all my strength, releasing her.

She hit hard, but rolled and sprang to her feet, facing off against me.

Ahmaia cried out in pain her hand going to her neck. That distracted me for the moment it took for Claw to sweep my legs out from under me.

I hit the ground hard, on my back.

She pounced.

I reacted on instinct, drawing my legs up and kicking her as she jumped upon me. She went flying, up and back, with a grunt. I spun to my feet as she landed — on her feet, like the cat she was — then she turned and tore a hole in the canvas wall of the tent, fleeing out into the night.

I followed, drawing my sword.

The pain of my arm and face had faded. My *Hero* spirit-gift had risen, even though I would be no hero tonight. Tonight, I was a spirit of vengeance.

Claw launched herself at me, and with a swipe of my sword, impassive and quick. I removed one of her hands.

She screeched a yowl of pain as the claws on her other hand skittered off my armor. She lashed out with her leg, another sweep, and I leaped just high enough to avoid it, landing close to her, my injured arm grasping her hair and yanking her head back.

"This is for Maverick," I hissed and ran my sword across her throat. I lifted her head up and back to let the blood flow faster, freer, and the fight went out of her quickly.

She went limp,

Dead.

Good. Something hard inside me hardened even more. It was done, I had my vengeance.

I tossed her body to the ground.

And only then became aware of the dozen or so men who'd come out from their tents, probably having heard Claw's scream. They'd seen me slay her. I whipped my sword down to shed the thick blood upon it and slowly spun my gaze to look at each of them in turn.

I can't imagine what I must have looked like in that moment, the look in my eyes, but every man around me cringed and fled.

Good.

I turned back to the tent... and Lord War's fist hit me solidly in the gut.

But unlike the time he'd punched me out of the air, and I'd gone flying, this time I was only knocked back a step as my armor seemed to disperse the hit, rippling like water when a stone is dropped into a still pond.

Lord War blinked, stunned. That had not been the reaction he'd expected.

I snapped a kick up to his face, which knocked him back... into Ahmaia's writhing cloth-arms. A moment later he was sucked into her magic pockets.

"You're bleeding," Ahmaia said, stoically.

I looked at my arm and shrugged. My *Hero* gift meant I was feeling little pain. I reached for my belly to gather some webbing to place over the wound. Even as I realized I was wearing armor over my belly-button and wouldn't be able to access my webbing, the metal of the armor... moved. It parted like flowing water once again, and I was able to gather some webbing into my hand. The armor closed up as I moved my hand away. I could definitely get used to this. I spread the webbing over my injured arm, stopping the blood for now. "I'll be well enough. There are more."

Ahmaia blinked then nodded. Midnight and the other Fey were finishing up with the two other Nobles who'd been asleep in the pavilion, and we spread out into the camp.

Claw's scream had woken others.

A man raced toward me, spear leveled, as another — in the form of a large cat — leaped at me.

Ahmaia's writhing cloth grabbed the leaping one out of the air, shunting him into her cloak as I deflected the spear thrust with my sword, driving it to one side of me before I lunged in and landed a strike on the man's leg, cutting deep. He fell screaming... for a moment... before he too was scooped into Ahmaia's cloak.

"That is five," Ahmaia said calmly. "I could take perhaps one or two more."

Just then, two younger Nobles ran at us. I recognized one

from my time at Silverveil and the Noble's Test, though I couldn't recall her name.

One veered into a tressym and flew at me, claws extended. Ahmaia sucked that one into her cloak as I engaged with the other. She used a whip, and it was clear she'd been trained in combat, but... not as relentlessly as I had. She struck and the whip wrapped itself around my sword arm. I released the blade to grab the leather whip, then pulled the woman in close. I caught her by the neck, then tossed her to Ahmaia, who gobbled her up. The woman hadn't even screamed, she'd been so surprised.

Midnight and the other Fey joined us after that.

"There are no more Nobles left here," Midnight said stoically. "We're done."

I nodded, feeling the fury of battle begin to ebb, my gift starting to fade. Pain would return soon.

"Let's go," I said and veered in mid-hop, caught by Ahmaia, who then tucked me away in her magical cloak.

Even having known this was my escape plan, I still wasn't prepared for the absolute darkness and the press of heavy, grainy fabric on all sides as I was held, unable to move.

Luckily, I had no reason to leave this place and relaxed as much as I could for the trip back to our camp.

Still, I was relieved to be released once back in Alvere's pavilion. We were the last to return.

Sparrow flew into my arms and embraced me. I could sense and feel her excitement and relief, the pounding of her heart. She held me for a long moment before releasing me. She then turned to Ant.

I saw the man, covered in blood, looking at his large hands, still dripping with gore.

"He tore Jaguar apart," Sparrow said with frightened

awe. "I knew he was strong, but..." her voice died. "He's still... not himself."

I could see that plainly.

"I'll talk with him, but not tonight." I raised my voice to say, "We have done what we needed to do. The war is over." Still, I felt no victory. "Get some rest. We still have lots to do." And perhaps that was why I didn't register the win. The battle here was over, but the war raging within the heart of Elista still needed to be dealt with...

...and I had no clue how I was going to do that.

CHAPTER 3

Fᴉɴ ʟᴇᴛ ᴏᴜᴛ ᴀ ᴘᴀɪɴꜰᴜʟ ɢʀᴜɴᴛ ᴀꜱ ᴛʜᴇ ʟᴀꜱᴛ ᴏꜰ ᴜꜱ ᴡᴇʀᴇ transported to the caves which were now my House's residence in Elista. Silence had told me all about them. They'd been dug out over a period of years by a man named Clam, forming an upper communal living area and a lower level with bedrooms. Above us, on the cliffs overlooking Dyren's Bay, was a cottage which Fin owned. Clam stayed there now, a reward for his hard work.

Speaking of Fin, the large man shouldn't have been exerting himself, but he'd insisted he was well enough to bring us all home. Fin was still wounded from the fight that had killed Maverick and the others, even though that had been nearly two weeks ago. Ant hadn't been able to heal him, he'd been tending to others who were more gravely wounded throughout the camp and was also exhausted. Though now, Ant was just... distant. He'd been consumed with revenge, but now that he had it, I think he felt hollow.

Like me.

Fin sat heavily in a comfortable looking chair and smiled. "See, I'm fine." Then he winced and shifted in the chair. "Almost." After a moment he added, "I'll just rest here until dinner. Once I've eaten, I'll limp down to my bed and sleep for a week."

"This is a strange yet amazing place," Alvere commented, looking around the large cave-like common area in awe. I had to agree. This was the first time I'd seen the underground hideout. It was impressive in its scale and the precision with which it had been carved from the bedrock here.

I was glad Alvere had been able to come with us. Leaving the command of his forces in the hands of his trusted generals and the Fey, he'd thought it safe to leave the front for a while, at least for one night... to be with me.

There was little left for us to do back in Vauphan. We'd tried to question the prisoners, but we weren't brutal like they were, wouldn't use violence to get our answers, which meant most of them weren't talking. We'd learned a little bit about what forces they were expecting for reinforcements over the coming weeks, but that was it. Lord War had, since being captured, remained as a wasp, we'd gotten nothing from him. Of all of them, he was the one I'd have been most willing to... hurt... a little, for information. I knew he wouldn't hesitate to do the same. But Ahmaia had stopped me. These people were under her care now and wouldn't be harmed. So, we had little to go on, which was frustrating.

I didn't want to think about that now. Today was meant to be a break from all that.

Crane, who'd been sent ahead to prepare for our arrival, walked briskly into view from the shadowy stairwell to one side of the large room.

She came directly to me. "It went well?" I could hear the concern in her voice, even as I caught her gaze moving around, counting us.

"Yes, Crane, we're all here." I sighed heavily. "The war in Vauphan is done for now." Lowering my voice so only she could hear, I added, "I have no clue what to do next."

She smiled sympathetically. "You'd be surprised how often Maverick said that."

I *was* surprised, and my shock must have shown, as her smile widened and she put an arm around me, comforting, motherly.

Drawing me aside from the others for a moment, she spoke softly. "He made certain he was always calm and sure in front of the rest of you, but I spent many sleepless nights with him while he paced, frantic and uncertain. He always found the right thing to do, the right things to say, as I'm sure you will too. And if you need me to stay up and watch you pace while we consider ideas, I'm here for you."

"I appreciate that, thank you," I said and hugged her close. "I'll probably take you up on that... tomorrow. Today, what remains of it, is for mending and celebration."

She nodded to that. "I'll have a feast prepared."

I hugged her again then moved away, going to Alvere. Kissing him lightly on the cheek, I whispered, "I have a few things I need to do. Make yourself at home. I'll find you later."

He smiled at that thought and I directed him into Sparrow's custody to be shown around.

Which left the largest item on my to do list: Ant.

I'd caught him heading down the stairs as soon as we'd arrived. I asked where his room was and went to it. There was no door to knock upon, only a heavy curtain, so I just entered.

I caught him mostly naked, perhaps readying for sleep, even though it was mid-afternoon. He saw me, paused with his pants halfway down his legs, then with a lifeless look in his eyes simply shrugged and continued.

"What?" he asked heavily, not seeming to care that he stood nude before me.

Wow, what a body. He was muscular and large, I'd seen him without a shirt before: his dark skin bulging with muscles, thick across his shoulders, chest, and arms. Now I saw his tight round butt, thick powerful legs and a long, swinging shaft that made my mouth dry up and my legs grow a little weak.

He sat heavily on his bed and I heard it creak.

"What?" he repeated, and I realized I'd been staring at him.

I sighed and — trying not to ogle him — went to sit on the bed, staying at the far end.

"You're hurting," I said, not really knowing how to have this conversation. "I can see it. Everyone can see it."

His head fell, his gaze upon the thick carpet over the stone floor. He leaned forward elbows on knees to hold his head as if the world itself weighed upon his shoulders. "She's gone," he said, voice hollow and pained. "I thought killing Jaguar would help, but... it didn't. There was a moment of satisfaction at making him suffer, but then..."

"I know," I confided, shifting just a bit closer to reach out my arm and stroke his back: his Oh-My-Spirits massive, V-shaped back. "I thought killing Lady Claw would make me feel better, and it did, for the briefest of moments, but now... I still feel hollow. Her death didn't bring Maverick back."

Ant nodded slowly. "What do I do?" He sounded so small and uncertain, so unlike himself.

I had no clue. "What do you need?" I asked.

"I... I..." He swallowed hard, voice becoming husky. "I never got to tell her how I felt. I... I think she knew, but I... I just wanted to say it, to say that I loved her and to say good-bye and... Spirits, I just want to hold her again."

I shifted closer still, though I couldn't reach across that broad back of his to hold him, hug him.

I had an idea.

"Close your eyes," I said softly. I didn't know if he complied or not, I couldn't see his face hidden behind his hands. "Now... hold me. Imagine I'm her. Tell me what you need to say."

He shifted, his face turning toward me. But he hadn't closed his eyes, and those dark orbs gazed at me for a long moment, tears on his cheeks.

I shifted close, brushing against him, feeling the heat and latent power of his form looming next to me. I lowered my voice, made it breathy and soft. I'd never fully sound like Amber, but this would be close.

"Close your eyes," I said again in that voice.

He winced, then sighed and shut his eyes.

He turned, reaching out, awkward but tender, to put a large, strong hand on my leg. I flushed a little at his touch, how he slid his hand up to my hip, then onto my waist and up, slowly, to my shoulder then my face, gently cupping my cheek.

"Amber?" He said, hopefully imagining her.

"I'm here," I said huskily, putting one of my hands on his cheek as he had with me.

He gave a shiver and I saw his face contort in pain and grief. "Oh, Spirits, I love you Amber!" He suddenly pulled me close, his other arm going around me. It was amazing how gentle he could be, how warm and loved I felt while held by those massive, muscled arms.

He wept as he poured his heart out to me. "I know you said we would always be casual, that it meant nothing, that you like my body and I liked yours and we should do something about that. You always had the right words, that casual caring grace and wonderful softness I needed. But... Oh Spirits, Amber." He sobbed for a moment before he continued, half choking on his words. "After our first time I was hooked. I needed you, I loved you. I should have said something, I should have told you. My heart is... I... You were everything to me."

"I know," I whispered. "I love you too." I was being her, but in that moment, I was also caught up in his words to me, even if they weren't to me.

"I was always a healer, but only of physical wounds. You were a balm on my soul, the caring and comfort I needed when the world got confused and torn. I love you so much!" He was blubbering now, holding me close. I held him as best I could, given his hugeness.

"I love you too," I whispered again.

Then, suddenly his lips were on mine, hard and needful, pushing and opening. I responded, caught up in his passion, surprised by how much I liked it. No man had ever been this rough with me, this hard and forward and...

He pulled back suddenly, eyes opening.

"I'm sorry," he said. "Legs, I..."

"You want to hold her one last time, be with her?"

"Yes, but—"

"Then do it. Be with me, like you would with her."

"But you can't—"

"It's my choice," I said, voice hushed but firm. Perhaps I was too caught up in his professions of love, but I was feeling desired and needed. From the corner of my eye, I caught his growing erection, so very tall and thick. A part of me was *very* curious what that would feel like. I'd never been with a man *that* big before.

I put a hand to his face, fingers tracing down over his eye-lids, encouraging his eyes to close. "Close your eyes," I said, voice trembling, mouth dry, swallowing hard. "And hold me, take me, one last time, my love."

"Yes," he breathed, voice choked with all his love and loss pouring out of him.

Then he moved in and I lost my breath in a savage kiss. He pushed me down to the bed, half over me. I felt the press of his weight upon me. His one hand sought the curve of my breast, over my dress, and gripped it hard. I gasped, or would have if I'd had any breath to give. My body responded to his need, aching, heating, throbbing with desire to have him close.

Then his lips left mine and I sucked in a long breath, only to have it gasped out again as his hand moved from my breast to my thigh, pushing up the skirt of my dress.

"Yes, take me," I whispered.

He gave a low chuckle. "You know I won't fit, not yet," he said as he shifted his body down, kneeling beside the bed, opening my legs to kiss my thighs, then... I gave another gasp as his tongue flicked over my clit. His lips pressed hard to my opening, as aggressive and driving with need as he'd been before. And it was exactly what I wanted. I pressed my hands to the tight curls of his dark hair, urging him closer. I felt my folds grow slick, my body flushed, heat pooling deep within me.

He worked with a probing tongue and biting teeth. I gasped and moaned when he slid a thick finger inside me, knowing just where to press and caress. He ravished me with a vigor the likes of which I had never known. I responded with groans and yelps, whispered words of encouragement and breathless gasps as he worked me up and up and up through the soft peak of one orgasm to the body-clenching, aching, screaming bliss of another.

I lay gasping in bewildered bliss, floating on a cloud of ecstasy. He moved over me and removed my dress with astonishing care. I hardly noticed. Then he rolled me onto my stomach, pulling me close. I tucked my knees up under me, against the edge of the bed as I felt his fingers slip into my folds, first one, then another, then a third, pushing inside me. That was *a lot,* almost too much. Yet as he probed and played inside me, I felt myself build to a new and — hopefully — even more amazing orgasm.

Then he removed his fingers, and I ached for the loss, whispering a plaintive, "No, please!"

But then I felt something large — the tip of his erection — press against me and I gasped. And as he pushed inside me, I breathed, "yes." My hands curled into the sheets, grabbing and kneading as he filled me. He was so big, just... wow! I now knew why he'd needed to work with three fingers for so long. Even with just his tip inside me I felt stretched and tight.

His massive hands grabbed my hips and I trembled with the anticipation of what would come next. He gave a series of slow, shallow thrusts, working a bit deeper each time as he grunted with pleasure. I let out a series of muffled screams into the sheets, biting them, eyes wide and body shaking as every slow and powerful inch of his erection pressed deeper and deeper inside me. Given how much he stretched me, I couldn't imagine the pressure and squeeze he must have felt.

And when he was as deep as he could be within me, there was a moment of pain, then an amazing spike of bliss. I jerked and shook for what seemed like an eternity as he simply sat fully within me. I couldn't tell — with my head pressing into his bed — but I didn't even think his entire length was inside me. I couldn't feel the press of his body to mine. He was just too long and large. And as a powerful wave of ecstasy rocked through me, I found myself going limp and relaxed. This extreme, yet serene plateau of pleasure was something I'd never felt before. I trembled faintly, waiting, desperately wanting to feel his aggressive thrusts. Spirits, I was overcome with bliss and he hadn't even really begun yet.

He stayed there, deep and large, as his hands moved up my sides, lifting me. I was pudding, melting in his grip as he easily raised me up to lean against him, hands under my breasts, feeling their weight for a moment before pressing and caressing them.

I let out a shuddering sigh of a moan and felt his body respond to the sound as he grunted and finally began slow, deep thrusts.

One hand moved down from my breasts to press to my clit as he moved within me and suddenly, I was on fire once again, stiff and stimulated beyond reason.

"I love you, Amber," Ant groaned as I felt a massive release shudder through me. I cried out a long, "yes!" and tried to move against him, shifting my hips to help with his thrusting as he began to pick up his pace.

I leaned my head back against the wide plateau of his shoulder and whispered, breathless: "Take what you need."

"Yes," he whispered in response. Then his hands were on my hips again, as we rocked and moved together, harder, faster.

Then...

With a cry of passion, he let loose upon me, thrusting with abandon.

Spirits Above!

Each slam of his massiveness inside me caused a tidal wave of pleasure to wash through me. I fell forward, landing on weak arms as I felt his immense strength pounding to infinite depths within me. My mouth and eyes opened wide in a silent scream of unimaginable bliss.

His pace quickened as he swelled inside me, stretching me to my limits. He was close.

My arms gave way and I fell forward onto my face. I reached one arm down to furiously rub my clit. I wanted to come with him.

With a roar and a final thrust, he planted himself deep within me and exploded in his bliss. As his hot surge rushed into me, I couldn't help but come with him, my body shuddering, hands pounding the softness of the bed over and over as I was rocked by his profound release.

I felt him slowly curl over me, arms wrapping around me as he wept against my back. This had been the release he'd needed, in more ways than one. He could finally begin to let Amber go and heal himself.

Eventually we slumped onto the bed together and he quieted. "Thank you," he whispered with a soft kiss on my shoulder. Then with a heavy sigh he said, "Good-bye, Amber."

CHAPTER 4

I STAGGERED, WALKING FUNNY WHEN I LEFT ANT'S ROOMS. I'D be sore down there for a little while, I suspected. I hoped for a bit of a rest before dinner, but alas, that was not to be. Sparrow stood outside my room. As the leader of the House, I got a slightly larger room than the rest, or so I'd been told. I hadn't actually seen it yet.

She spoke softly to me with a faint smile. "Silence and the prince are inside... ah... getting to know each other."

I raised my brow at that.

Sparrow, ever-perceptive, then cocked her head in a slightly bird-like manner. "You seem... different."

I had nothing to hide from her, or the others. I'd tell them the truth about where I'd been. "I spent some time with Ant. He needed to let go of Amber, and now he has. But to do that I told him to imagine I was her, to give her what he needed to give her. And he gave it to me... hard. I'm going to be sore for a while."

Sparrow blinked, those large forest-green eyes going wider still as she gave a shy-shocked smile. "Oh." She looked away, blushing. "I have to admit, I've always been curious about him."

"I can tell you all about it, or you can be his next paramour if you like." Though she was even smaller than I was. "*If* you like your pleasure to be on the verge of punishment."

She blushed deeper. "I... don't think so."

I shrugged and stepped in close to whisper, "You should try it at least once before you make up your mind." Then I kissed her cheek. "Now, I'm curious what Silence and Alvere are up to."

What I saw when I entered was the last thing I expected: Silence and Alvere kissing softly, arms around each other, sitting on my bed.

Despite my soreness, this scene caused a rather instant arousal to rush through me. "Oh!" I breathed.

They stopped kissing to turn to me, but kept their arms around each other.

"Silence was... initiating me into your little harem," Alvere said, a bit flushed.

"Given your desire for Sparrow and willingness to be with her..." Silence shrugged. "I was curious what this might be like." That made sense, since I knew that Silence's only true example of love growing up, had been two men.

"And?" I asked, also curious.

They looked at each other and I saw something kindle there, even if it was uncertain and undefined as of yet. I couldn't blame them: they were both attractive men with a healthy dose of curiosity and an abundance of love.

Alvere responded, still looking longingly into Silence's eyes. "We... think we'd like to find out more?"

Silence nodded to that.

Alvere turned to me, "But for now we can focus on you."

"No," I said quickly raising my hands. "Actually, please continue." I could get behind just watching this.

Both raised their brows in question.

"I'm a little tired and sore right now," I said, fully meaning to explain, but Sparrow jumped in first.

"She got Ant through his grief for Amber by allowing him to imagine Legs was Amber, and giving him one last release with his beloved."

Silence's and Alvere's brows rose even higher. "But he's huge," Silence said in awe.

Alvere nodded, "Ah, hence... tired and sore. Understood." He turned back to Silence. "What do you think? Would you like more... with me?"

Silence considered for a moment, then nodded and they rose, hand in hand, making to leave.

"No, stay!" I said quickly. I hadn't told them my intention to watch. "I... want to..."

"Watch?" Alvere said with a grin.

I nodded, growing more heated and excited at the thought.

Alvere turned to Silence, a question in his glance, and Silence shrugged and nodded. The two then came together again, embracing and kissing.

Spirits Within! That is so hot!

I skirted around them to my — quite large — bed. That seemed appropriate since I had a lot of people I wanted to share it with. Sparrow came with me, sitting next to me as I reclined on some pillows, holding me close.

I could get used to this.

I watched the gradual kindling of passion between the two men, soft kisses slowly deepening to tongue-play, then hungry, open mouths. It was one of the most sensuous and stimulating things I'd ever seen.

I shivered with a surge of bliss when Sparrow suddenly kissed my neck, her hand reaching up over my dress to gently cup one of my breasts.

She whispered: "I'll be gentle." And her kisses moved over my cheek and into my hair.

Turning my head, I captured her lips with mine, savoring their plump sweetness as the heat within me bubbled up to a strong simmer. When I drew back, our hot breath mingled between us.

"Just relax," Sparrow whispered, and I did. I turned back to watch the boys as Sparrow spent her time with slow soft kisses over my neck and ear, into my hair and down over my cheek.

Silence had his shirt off now, Alvere's was in the process of being removed. Once it was off, their lips met again, their hands roaming the exposed expanse of nearly twin bodies. Silence was leaner, muscles long and wiry on his limbs. His chest was flat, just beginning to swell with muscle. Across his abdomen were a series of well-defined and squarish abs.

Ant's abs were like... fresh, plump buns, hot from the oven.

Where had that thought come from?

Auwei giggled. *I've had a man like Ant before, only once, and I may have thought of him like that: one big sweet dessert, too rich to have often, but nice to have once in a while, when you want to be filled up more than usual.*

Wow, really?

Oh yes. He was... something else, but I must admit, your Ant is even more. I very much enjoyed that experience, thank you.

You're welcome, you don't have to live with the soreness afterward.

I do feel what you feel.

Oh... right.

Now, Auwei said, and I could hear the breathy eagerness in her voice, *back to the steamy buffet in front of us. This, just watching, is new for me too.*

And for me. Aren't they just beautiful together?

Indeed. Now let me watch in peace.

So, I went back to gazing longingly at my men. Compared to Silence Alvere was a bit larger, his chest and arms and shoulders more rounded, though is abdomen was the same flat, chiseled perfection.

Silence removed Alvere's breeches and I gasped as his erection was freed, leaping up before him. Silence kissed down Alvere's perfect abbs, then knelt, stroking that perfect shaft, kissing the tip softly.

Blessed Spirits! I hadn't expected them to go this far!

Alvere gasped as his erection visibly swelled. Yeah, Ant's massive manhood was a sinful and slightly painful pleasure, but Alvere's was perfection. Just the right size and length.

Sparrow softly bit my earlobe, and I gasped with a surge of pleasure. I suddenly wanted more from the woman and shifted away and to my knees so I could lift off my dress.

I caught Sparrow doing the same from the corner of my eye and heard Alvere's new gasp. His erection seemed to grow larger still as he gazed over at me... just before Silence took him full into his mouth and Alvere's eyes rolled back. He put a hand to the wall to steady himself.

Sparrow pushed herself against my back, her soft breasts, nipples hardened with her own arousal, pressed to me as her hands moved around me, slowly and softly caressing my abdomen, then up to my breasts to gently cup and knead. My own nipples were rigid and standing proud and needed little in the way of further stimulation.

The men had shifted, Alvere's back against the wall, head back, hands softly sliding through Silence's mouse-brown hair as Silence's head began to move quicker, his one hand on Alvere's thigh, the other gently cupping and stroking his sack.

"Enough," Alvere breathed and urged Silence's head away. Alvere's hands motioned and helped Silence stand and their lips met feverishly again for a moment before Alvere spun them and pinned Silence to the wall. "Your turn," he breathed and was quickly kneeling, removing Silence's breeches.

Alvere greedily plunged his mouth over Silence's throbbing erection, his grip hard and stroking. It was Silence's turn to gasp. Then his gaze rose and saw me and he gasped again, mouth hanging open in awed desire.

"I won't... I can't... Oh!" Silence groaned as his hands curled into Alvere's black hair and his eyes rolled back with what I guessed was an unexpected release. Yet Alvere continued his work, moving over Silence's twitching length with rapid intensity. "Yes." Silence drew the word out as his gaze caught mine. "Yes," he repeated, and I was just a bit surprised to have Sparrow's fingers lightly trace over my folds in that moment.

I'd lost track of her caresses while watching Silence's bliss, but now I was keenly aware of her subtle movement.

"Gently," I reminded her.

"I know," she whispered, hot breath on my ear. She was being so very tender, so much so that her featherlike brushes made me want more. Her other hand joined the first and stroked the insides of my thighs with urgent, but careful caresses.

Silence, in the meantime, had gone a little slack, now taking long, deep breaths, moving his gaze from Alvere to me. "By all the Spirits! That was... oh!" Silence breathed as

Alvere moved away. Silence was still semi-erect but clearly spent.

Alvere himself looked flushed, ready for his own release, his erection still straining before him. He stepped away from Silence and breathed his own "oh." He laughed a little, clearly giddy. "Well, that was... new."

Silence let out a bit of a laugh as well. "Yes. I was... very excited. Can you blame me?" He motioned to me. Alvere turned to me and bit his lip.

"No, I can't."

"Shall I return the favor?" Silence said as the two of them came together for another series of deep kisses. Silence's hand sought and stroked Alvere's erection, which looked ready to burst.

"No, I have another idea, if you're up for it," Alvere said when they separated. "Something that will allow us to both watch our beloved Legs being pleasured."

Silence raised a brow, then his eyes widened and he nodded. He'd figured out what Alvere was saying, even though I hadn't.

Alvere's going to enter him from behind, Auwei filled me in.

"Do you have oil?" Alvere asked me as he quickly went to the single drawer in the nightstand next to the bed. I'd never been in this room before, so I had no clue. He opened the drawer and breathed a sigh — mixed with relief and anticipation — as he pulled out a small glass container filled with golden liquid. He removed the stopper and smelled it nodding. "Great!"

Apparently, this room came well stocked.

Silence had moved to the edge of the bed and Alvere returned to him, pouring a little of the liquid onto his fingers, reaching around behind Silence. Alvere handed over the small container and Silence also doled out a bit, stroking it onto Alvere's swollen erection. Both men were flushed and breathing heavily, gasping just a bit as they worked upon each other in preparation.

I hadn't known how much I wanted to see this, until now.

Anal sex can be very stimulating for men... women as well, if you're ever interested, Auwei said.

I hadn't been interested before, but with my heart racing, I was suddenly curious.

When they finally shifted, Alvere moving behind the other man, I could barely breathe, throat tight with thrilled anticipation. Silence gasped in what looked like a mix of pain and pleasure as I guessed Alvere carefully inserted himself.

Silence moaned and leaned forward onto the bed, as Alvere, hands on Silence's hips, moved slowly, pushing deeper. The prince's eyelids fluttered, mouth agape, body shuddering: lost to bliss.

And Sparrow, prescient as ever, chose that moment to *finally* brush my clit. I let out a surprised cry as my body tensed, suddenly very ready for more.

"You can be just a little harder," I breathed between gasps, and she applied just a bit more pressure as her fingers slid around my folds and stroked my ragingly sensitive nub.

I raised my hands to my breasts, kneading and tweaking to add to my pleasure.

Poor Sparrow, the remaining three of us were all about to orgasm, and she was content to passively pleasure me. I'd have to reward her for that later. But then my mind wasn't on her anymore. The beautiful men before me were both gasping and grunting as Alvere picked up his pace, thrusting hard and needful into Silence, who was also near to another peak it seemed. He fell to his elbows, arms weak, and one arm disappeared, probably to stroke himself as the three of us shook and shuddered toward an ultimate release.

I was more than ready. Sparrow's hands worked miracles, pressing hard enough to get me ragingly hot and bothered, while not so hard as to cause any pain to my aching entrance.

Alvere came first, crying out with a final desperate lunge into Silence. Silence also cried out, but it wasn't until a moment later when Silence's eyes rolled back and he jerked and tensed with another cry.

And I couldn't help myself. My beautiful men were so hot in their mutual pleasuring and Sparrows fingers were so nimble and quick, that I too cried out, body tensing and convulsing as I squeezed my own breasts in the throes of one of the most pleasurable orgasms I'd ever had. So very different than what I'd had with Ant, and yet just as powerful and intense.

I even heard Sparrow moan a little as she withdrew her fingers.

When Sparrow released me, I collapsed onto the bed. She remained kneeling, hungry eyes devouring me as she pleasured herself. It wasn't long before she too was crying out in bliss.

Alvere collapsed over Silence, kissing his back between heavy breaths. After a moment he looked up at me and Sparrow and softly stroked Silence's hair as he said, "I think I could get used to this."

CHAPTER 5

I FELT ENERGIZED.

After that stunningly sexy encounter in my room, our little troop had joined the rest of the house for a wonderful and filling meal. Alvere, Sparrow, Silence, and I had shared furtive glances and secret smiles as we ate.

After dinner, everyone gathered in the common area, a fire raging in the large hearth. It was time to talk about next steps.

"I have a crazy idea," I said as I paced back and forth in front of the fire.

"Why do I get the feeling all our briefings are going to start with that phrase," Princess mock-whispered to Foggy. He gave a snort of a laugh. I couldn't help but laugh as well, and others followed suit.

"Perhaps they will," I said in a playfully threatening sort of way. "We'll find out. But for now, I have probably the craziest idea of them all." I stopped pacing. "I want to kidnap the queen."

I stood there, waiting for the expected shocked gasps

and protests. Instead, I saw my house slowly nodding and grudgingly accepting this idea.

"We need to know what's going on, and the Royal House is clearly involved," Crane said. "Either she must know what's happening, or we'll find out if she's completely unaware, which seems unlikely. Yes, this seems a logical course of action, though I have no clue how we'd pull it off."

"I might have an idea," Dove said, voice hesitant. My sister still hadn't fully recovered from the betrayal of her former lover, Lord Hale. It seemed he'd only been seeing her to get to me, and when he'd turned on us both, it had devastated my sister. She was better now than she had been, but still a little deferential in her new House... My House. As my older sister, it must be odd to have me as her House Leader.

"I'm all ears," I said. "I had no set plan in mind, just a knowledge that, as Lady Crane said, we need to know what the queen knows."

"The Spring Festival will be in a few days," Dove said. If it happens as usual, then the queen will lead a parade of Nobles through the capital, from her House to the Great Square."

"So, she'll be out in the open," I said.

"And surrounded by Nobles," Lady Crane added sourly. "How will we ever take her unnoticed?

Dove nodded. "That would be the downside." She sighed. "Perhaps that wasn't the best idea."

"No, I think we can work with this," I said, beginning to pace again. "The trouble with the queen has been her seclusion these past few weeks. In order to get to her, we'd have to search the Owl Estate. The chances of getting in and getting out without encountering some of her Nobles would be highly unlikely anyway. This way, at least we know where she'll be and when."

"If we wait until after the parade and her speech in the square, she may retire back to her House with only a few guards." Dove shrugged.

"I wish..." I silenced myself. I'd been about to say I wished that Amber was still here. Her power to influence the minds of others would have been handy. But despite Ant's turning the corner and starting to let her go, I didn't think he'd want to hear that right now. So, I threw the question out to the group. "How do we get her away from a few Nobles and guards without harming anyone?" We didn't really know who was a part of this intrigue and who wasn't, and the idea was to kidnap the queen without casualties.

"Fin could pop in and grab her and pop out?" Silence said looking over at the large man. Fin had lost some of his girth these last few days, and he was still covered in bandages. He didn't look like he'd be up for much, not right away at least.

Fin grunted and shrugged. He was half asleep as it was. If we were going to use Fin at all we'd need to make sure he was well recovered.

"Good idea... though we also need to account for Lord Hale. If he's with the queen that could mess things up for us. I know he can stop people from veering and cut them off from their Lumani, what I don't know is if he can stop a person's spirit-gift. I'm guessing he can't, since Midnight and I were able to use ours while close to him, but... there is a slim chance he can, but has to concentrate or somehow activate that power and he didn't at that time because he just didn't know we had spirit gifts." I shrugged. "For the moment, let's assume he can. If so, we need some way to neutralize him and any others safely."

"There has to be a way," Crane said, looking into the fire in thought. "Perhaps if we each share what we can do, that might spark something?" She looked around. "I know we've done this many times, but I think it might help to do it again."

Alvere shrugged. "You all may have done it many times before, but I haven't been here. So, I'll go first. I can control cloth," he said, then blinked, head slowly tilting to one side. He was clearly stuck on some thought. For those of the House who hadn't known that Alvere was half-Fey and had some of their abilities, this statement had opened some eyes.

Alvere turned to me. "You know, if you asked for some help from the Fey, they might be able to take some others out of the picture. Those like me could potentially stop anyone in regular clothes. And if there were guards in armor, a few of those who control metal could help as well." He shrugged. "I can ask them if you like."

That might be very useful. I had hoped to do this with just the members of my House, but a little outside help might go a long way. Certainly, it would be something the Nobles wouldn't be used to fighting against. I'd seen how powerful and useful the Fey could be during our raid on the Elistan camp. The way Ahmaia had scooped people up and hidden them somehow, in the "pockets" of her cloak, was amazing.

"That's a great idea, thank you Alvere."

"If that fails you could just kiss everyone," Foggy said with a wide grin.

I didn't understand what he meant for a long moment... then remembered my toxic lips, my ability to stun people. I laughed. "We'll save that as a backup option."

"And what do we do with the queen once we have her?"

Midnight asked softly. "Do you truly expect her to spill all her secrets?"

"No, not really, but—"

"Then what's the point of kidnapping her?" Trust Midnight to get right to the heart of things.

I thought for a moment before answering. "My hope is that once we start questioning her, it will become apparent whether she knows nothing of the events happening around her, or she does know and isn't doing anything about them. I think those will be two very different responses, even if she isn't all that talkative. That alone will tell us a lot. And if she does know something and is willing to talk, then... that's even more."

Midnight sighed. "That's fair." She shook her head slowly. "I don't know why, but I suspect she's not the one behind all of this. It's just a hunch. I guess we'll see."

Time for specifics. "The mission team will be Alvere, myself, Fin, and the Fey, if they're willing. If not, we'll re-evaluate. The rest of you, make a room ready for the queen, we're about to have guests."

"Do we know if the queen has a spirit-gift?" Silence asked looking around.

A good question. I surely didn't.

"The trouble with most spirit-gifts is that they are personal. Most people don't share that they have them, except perhaps to those in their own House." Crane's tone was hard. "She may have one, but the public, even the other Noble Houses, haven't been told of it. We have to plan for... anything."

"Do that," I said.

"I'd like to come along on the mission," Midnight said. "I can stay behind, see what trouble we stir up, who reacts and how."

"A good idea. You're in." I looked around. "Anything else?"

No one said anything.

I sought out Ant after the meeting as people went to prepare. He hadn't said anything and had been avoiding eye contact. "How are you feeling?" I asked tentatively. The dark skin of his cheeks flushed as he looked at me, then quickly away. "I'm doing a lot better, thank you. I... just... You..." He cleared his throat. "Are you well? I was... rough."

I didn't laugh, even though I wanted to. I did flush a little myself as I smiled. "I'm tough, I can take a beating," I said remembering all the moments of my time with him. "I'm a bit sore, but I'll heal." I put a hand on his massive shoulder. "And if you ever need me, I'm here for you." I didn't really know what I was saying. Did I want more rough, powerful sex with this amazing man?

I can answer that, Auwei said with a chuckle. *Yes, yes you do. Just not often.*

Ant looked at me then. "You want more?" And the interest, the desire that kindled in his eyes sent a thrill through me, heat pooled low in my abdomen, making my sore parts tingle.

"Do you?" I asked, curious. No one else was around, so I was open with him. "I'm not a one-man woman, I think you know that. I seem to have a growing harem of those who I'm with. That's just who I am, and I'm not going to change that. But if you're well with that, then..." I lowered my voice to a sensuous, heavy whisper. "I could submit myself for a little punishment every now and then."

He grinned, while still looking a bit concerned. "Is that what it felt like? Punishment?"

"The most pleasurable pain I've ever felt," I breathed. I slipped my hand behind his neck and urged him down to me. He let me move him and leaned down for a quick nip of a kiss, his lips hard and hungry.

"I'd like to be with you again," he whispered.

"And I you. It's set. I'll let the others know there's a new member of the Loving Legs Club." I just made that name up on the spot and frowned at how silly it sounded.

"I'm not sure I'm up for others being with us," Ant said, honestly. "But... perhaps... I could try it. Once."

"It's good to be open to new experiences." I pulled him down for another kiss.

We drew apart after that. The heat within me lasted as I went back to my room. Alvere, Silence, and Sparrow were waiting for me there.

"What's this?" I asked, blinking in mock innocence.

"We just wanted to make sure you slept well," Alvere said.

"So, you're going to tire me out?" I shrugged. "Works for me." I drew into their loving arms, adding, "Oh, and I had a chat with Ant. He wants to be with me too, occasionally. How does everyone feel about that?"

"You know we only want you to be happy," Sparrow said, before her soft lips touched mine. The two men murmured their agreement as they pressed close... and began to show me just how happy they wished me to be.

As I slipped into a pleasantly contented sleep that night... I casually wondered if anyone else in my House might eventually join my little — but ever-growing — harem.

CHAPTER 6

AHMAIA AGREED TO HELP US. WITH HER CAME ELVI, A TINY Fey woman who could work with stone, and Eorthan, a stocky Fey man who controlled metal. Eorthan was the one who'd made my special armor, and I took a moment to thank him profusely for his amazing work. As for Elvi, it was thought that since the streets of the capital were made of stone she might be able to literally stop people in their tracks if needed.

Ahmaia insisted that Alvere not come. He was upset, but conceded to her argument that he was too significant to risk on a mission. As the king of Vauphan, fighting for his own country was one thing, but this was another. There was a vehemence and sternness in Ahmaia's insistence, and before we left, I took her aside for a quick chat.

"You're his mother, aren't you? Or a relative?" I asked, straight to the point. She didn't look old enough to be his mother, but I'd learned that Fey aged differently than humans.

She stared intently at me with her rose-gold eyes. "Yes," she said simply. "You are very astute."

"He doesn't know, does he?" From how he talked about his Fey parentage I'd gotten the feeling he'd never met his real mother.

"No." Her gaze never wavered when she asked, "Will you tell him?"

I smiled slightly. "It's not my place." Though I was curious. "Why... haven't you?"

I saw the slight twitch of her blue-pale skin at her jaw. I'd hit a nerve. "It will not help him. He had his parents. They raised him, I did not. He is a king and the Uniter. He will bring Fey back to the world. I... would only hinder him."

"I don't think so," I said. "I think having a parent, even one he's never known until now would only help him. But that's your choice to make. I will say nothing."

She nodded stiffly. "Thank you." She seemed about to leave but hesitated and said, "Our sages have seen things about you." She smiled. "I cannot tell you what. For that might influence your decisions. But... I know from what I have witnessed that you love my son. Thank you for that," she said softly. "Take care of him."

"I will," I said, curious as The Deepest Pits what those sages had seen. First the mistweaver had seen things about me and now this. What was a girl to think? I could get a complex, thinking I was someone important. Luckily, I knew better. Important or not, I was me, and I always would be. I'd do what I always did, and if that fulfilled someone's prophecy, good for them.

I met up with Fin, Midnight, and the Fey. We were all dressed as commoners, in concealing apparel which wouldn't seem out of place. Fin transported us to Ana's farm. Ana, being Maverick's sister, had to be told what had happened to her brother. Midnight offered, but I knew I had to do it.

When I did, Ana's features hardened, taking the news stoically.

"I always knew his life would be dangerous, or at least more dangerous than mine. I'm... glad he passed fighting for what was right, for his country... even if it was against his country." She shed a few tears and embraced me while I felt awful. I hadn't told her Maverick had died helping me, nor the gory specifics of his death, but both of those things still haunted me.

We walked from Ana's farm into the city, taking a room in a rundown tavern in the slums on the other side of the river. The Festival began tomorrow, and we'd be in place when it happened.

Midnight scouted during the night. We were all up before dawn to catch a ferry across the river and claim our spot near the square, a flat roofed building which would give us a good vantage point to watch the queen's speech. The building was behind the stage which had been erected for that purpose. We'd only see the back of the queen. But then... we weren't there for the speech. The building did have a good view of all of the exits the queen might take from that stage, assuming she left off the back and wanted to remain out of sight as she returned to her House. As the morning wore on, it even became clear exactly which route she'd take. We were in luck. We watched guards clear people out of the alley right next to the building we'd claimed. We'd have a perfect view of the queen — and whoever was with her — as they left. The guards stationed men along the alley and at both ends, so no one would use the road.

Our first problem came when three guards climbed up

to our rooftop and found us. Luckily, they didn't know who we were, just thought we were peasants there to claim our spot early.

"This roof is off limits, find somewhere else to view the queen's speech," the one guard growled. We could take these three easily, the trouble was... if we did, someone might notice that they'd gone missing.

Fin stepped forward and spoke in a voice I'd never heard from him before, a full-on, back-woods peasant drawl. "Sorry, mas'ers," he said holding up his hands. "We's jus' trying to get a peep at the queen. We don't think no'un woul' want dis place. We won't be no bother. If'n you're gonna watch the queen from up here, we coul' jus' watch with you."

The guard blinked, and I could see him trying to parse Fin's words. "Sorry lad, but no one can be up here. Now if you hurry, perhaps you can find some other rooftop. Just, go on now."

That hadn't worked.

For a moment I considered trying to subdue the guards and take their clothes. That way anyone down below would only see guards, but... I was the only one who *might* possibly fit into one of their uniforms. Fin was too big and the others were all too small.

We all stood there, awkwardly — guards and us both — for a long moment. My *Hero* gift rose within me. It wanted to fight, to remove these impediments to my plan. But I resisted that pull.

Any thoughts? I asked Auwei. *I'm desperate.*

Just one, but I'm not sure if you'll like it.

I'm all ears. Anything goes.

It'll be easier for me to show you.

Do it!

Auwei swept through me, taking control. The next moment, I walked forward in a sexy swagger. All three guards watched me. I wasn't even dressed in anything particularly provocative, but that was the trick to Auwei's walk. I'd never quite learned to move like this. I'd always been a bit of a rough-and-tumble girl, not the flirty type, but Auwei had been all sorts of people and this walk, though it felt extremely odd, was doing the trick. The guards seemed mesmerized by my swaying hips and long legs and shifting shoulders.

Trust me it's not your shoulders they're looking at.

I reached the first guard, pressed myself against him, wrapped my arms around his neck and laid a kiss upon his lips. I could tell he enjoyed it. I felt his body respond, his mouth open... then... he went stiff.

Oh, right!

I moved away from him, leaving him seemingly stunned, to kiss the second guard. Apparently, Midnight caught the first one as he fell forward, lowering him gently to the ground. The third guard had the benefit of seeing the other two go stiff and fall. He backed a step away from me before I reached him. Still, somehow, he melted at my kiss, responding before going stiff himself.

I stepped back, catching the last guard as he fell.

Too easy, especially with your body. Auwei was purring with glee.

Thanks?

It's the legs, they make all the difference in that walk.

Oh...

She giggled as she receded from controlling me.

"And what did that get us?" Ahmaia asked coming over to us.

Yes, what did that gain us? I asked Auwei

Then I repeated her answer verbatim to Ahmaia. "Now those guards are going to be seen up here, guarding things and no one should bother us. Just lean the men up against the side walls so others can see them, and from below, they may seem a bit stiff, but hopefully no one will notice."

Ahmaia cocked her head to one side. "That might work. How long will they remain like this?"

"About an hour."

"Will that be enough time?"

It was just past dawn and the queen's speech was to be mid-morning. "No, I'll have to kiss them again from time to time to keep it up."

"You have a... stunning kiss?"

I laughed. "Yeah... some time remind me to tell you how Alvere and I met."

She raised a brow at that. "I have time now, it seems."

So we did.

I told her.

The shocked-strangled sound she made when I spoke of kissing and abducting Alvere was one of the oddest sounds I'd ever heard.

As the morning drew on, crowds gathered, the square below filled, and others could be seen on rooftops. We had to keep low, as there was a contingent of guards on the roof on the other side of the alley. They called over to our guards every now and then and Fin and Eorthan did a decent job of mimicking the guard's voices to call back. Luckily no one else came up to the roof to check on these three.

Then it was time.

We spotted the queen and her escorts moving down the cleared path, which had been made for the parade toward the platform. The queen's white-blond hair was easy to spot, flowing free, waving slightly behind her as she walked. With her was her second, Lady Merlin, a small woman with an intensity of nervous energy. But my eyes were drawn to the massive form of Lord Hale, even larger than Ant. I suddenly seethed with rage, remembering what he'd done to me, but more importantly, what he'd done to Dove.

"I'm going to kill you," I whispered.

Ahmaia looked at me askance. "The queen?" she whispered.

"No, the large man behind her. He... hurt my sister and tried to have me killed. He's marked."

"Ah... it seems you've marked many people."

No, only him and Lady Claw, who I'd already dealt with.

What I found even more interesting was the woman Lord Hale had on his arm. I knew her. Her name was Lady Swan, but I'd known her as Cedar at Silverveil. She'd never liked me. It didn't surprise me at all that she and Hale had hooked up. Also in the procession were a few more from the Royal House as well as other Nobles. Of note were Lady Silvermane of Pegasus House, the queen's daughter. We knew she was involved somehow, though perhaps not entirely willingly. It was her second, Lord Horn — Hale's father — who was much more involved and probably influencing her to help. Yet, I had trouble believing that she knew nothing. If her mother, the queen, was involved, Silvermane would have to know something.

Another spike through my heart was seeing Lady Skyfire, of House Wyvern, marching with the queen. I'd always admired her and didn't want to believe she would be involved with any of this. In truth, she might not be, but might just be a pawn, supporting the queen here, but not knowing what was truly happening. I wanted to believe that, but I had to assume everyone was against me right now.

The queen took the stage and began her speech.

Someone used magic to enhance her voice so everyone could hear; perhaps that was her spirit-gift?

My heart thundered in my ears — anxious for what was to come — and I hardly heard the speech. The queen finished far too quickly — though that was probably just my perception — then she was moving down the stairs at the back of the stage and heading for our laneway.

My heart pounded all the harder. I was going to do this. I was going to kidnap the queen.

I looked to the others, wondering if they were as scared as I was. Yet they all looked at me with certainty. They believed I could do this.

I smiled to reassure them, then we joined hands with Fin, ready to jump down.

This was it.

CHAPTER 7

WE APPEARED BEHIND THE QUEEN'S PARTY. THE ONLY NOBLES with her now were her second Lady Merlin, Lord Hale, and Lady Swan. They, along with half a dozen guards, were moving quickly down the laneway. Eorthan made a motion sweeping outwards to the side with both of his hands. Anyone in armor was suddenly flying to one side, which included Lord Hale. That left the queen, Merlin, and Swan.

Elvi, the stone wielder, made a motion pushing down with her hands. Merlin and Swan were suddenly trapped calf-deep in the stone street.

Fin Jumped to the queen and vanished with her.

The guards lining the street were only now beginning to react. My *Hero* gift surged. I'd hidden a short-sword under my commoner's clothes and already had it in hand. I reacted faster than they did, moving to protect our group. Midnight did the same, but unseen. Ahmaia was throwing about guards with her cloth-arms.

We only had to last a moment or two before...

Fin returned.

We rushed to him and a moment later were back in our cliffside hideout.

"We did—" My words cut off when I saw Alvere catch the queen as she collapsed. She had both hands at her throat. "What...?"

I rushed to kneel next to Alvere, who cradled the queen in his arms.

"You've killed me!" the queen hissed, as she strained to gasp in a breath.

"It started as soon as Fin arrived with her," Alvere said, just as shocked as I was.

The queen's desperate, wild-eyed gaze found me and she let out a sort of coughing laugh. "Of course," she croaked. She reached up to grasp my arm, her nails digging into my flesh. "You can't save me, but... you need... to..." She struggled more and more to get air. Her words became quieter and more frantic. "Merlin..." a long gasp, as her eyes rolled back. "...is..." I couldn't even tell if she was breathing now, her body convulsing as if trying to breathe, but getting no air. "M—ahhh..." The last of her air escaped with that last attempt at speech and she went limp. Her hand fell away from my arm, slapping the floor. Then, the faintest bit of mist slipped out from her lips.

"What in The Blackest Pits!" I hissed.

What had just happened?

"A mistweaver did this," Crane said crouching next to me.

"Sorry, what?" I hadn't heard that right. I couldn't have heard that right.

"A mistweaver," Crane repeated.

"We killed the mistweaver. *I* killed the mistweaver."

Crane shrugged. "That last puff of mist leaving her, that's what seals it. A mistweaver did this, some sort of curse.

Perhaps something to the effect of: if she left the capital she'd die? It may have been something lingering from the one you killed, but we can't discount the option that another is out there."

"Another mistweaver?" I'd nearly died fighting the first one. I would have died if Ant hadn't been there to patch me up afterward.

My mind spun out of control. None of this made sense. I'd tried to kidnap the queen and instead I'd killed her, because of some mistweaver's curse?

"What was it she said at the end?" Alvere said laying the body down gently. "Merlin is Ma...?" He looked at me. "Merlin was her second, yes?"

I nodded, though I wasn't really paying attention to what he was saying. My heart swarmed with guilt and fear. I sat back heavily on my rump, putting a hand to my head.

"Perhaps Merlin is a mistweaver?" Crane suggested.

"Or Merlin is the master? Perhaps she's the one behind all of this?" Alvere offered.

"Either way, it would suggest Merlin is the person we need to watch," Crane agreed.

Their words faded, growing distant. I didn't want to be here. I couldn't be here. I couldn't believe another choice I'd made had killed another potentially innocent person, though we didn't know that. We didn't know anything. My whole plan had hinged on getting some information from the queen. What did we have now?

No information and a dead body.

I got up and walked away, then ran. I was in my bed, face-down in a pillow before I knew it, hot and bitter tears wetting the softness against my face.

I felt a gentle hand on my back, moving in slow circles and knew who it was instantly. Sparrow. She asked nothing, said nothing, she simply sat there, softly rubbing my back until I'd cried myself out and was ready to do something other than weep.

My thoughts were still a mess of confusion and swirling uncertainty. My emotions were bunched into a tight ball of frustration, regret, and dismay.

I rolled onto my side and looked up at Sparrow's kind face. Her forest-green eyes were shaded with concern. She smiled softly, her soft cheeks rising. Her hand came to my face and swept some hair from my brow.

"What do you need?" she asked softly.

My voice warbled and broke as I said, "I don't know how to be strong right now. I need to be strong for the House, but..."

She nodded. "We understand," she whispered. "No one was expecting this. It's a shock. We're all trying to come to terms with it. We know it's not your fault."

But it *was* my fault. One of my first plans as leader of his House and I'd gotten a woman killed. I'd gotten *the queen* killed.

"I don't know how to do it," I said, sniffing as tears threatened again.

"Do what?"

"Live with all these lives, these deaths. I... I can't. What if..." I couldn't go on as tears flooded back. I'd been thinking *what if you had died, or Silence, or Alvere, or Ant?*

And then it occurred to me that I was favoring certain members of my House over others. I'd feel doubly guilty if Princess or Foggy or Midnight or anyone else died, because I hadn't been as concerned for them as I had for some others. That prompted tears of shame, to add to my tears of grief.

Sparrow laid herself down gently upon me, embracing me awkwardly.

"I don't think it gets easier," she said softly.

Not what I wanted to hear.

"But I'll always be here to comfort you, and if not me, one of the others. That's the point of having a House. We're family."

Family... Dove! I'd completely forgotten about my sister! That spurred another wave of heaving sobs. And Sparrow held me through all of it. Eventually we shifted and ended up with her laying on her back, taking the place of my pillow as I lay with my head upon her chest. She held me close, stroking my hair.

It was a while before my tears stopped again. By then I was getting quite hungry. My stomach rumbled. I hadn't eaten since early that morning.

Sparrow gave a few breaths of a laugh. "Hungry?"

"Yes."

"Silence?" she called out and the young man was in my room a moment later.

"Yes?" he said, brown eyes filled with concern.

"Food?"

He nodded and left.

"Was he just waiting outside?" I asked, shocked at how quickly he'd entered after being called.

"Yes," Sparrow whispered. "He wanted to come in with me, but I thought that might be a bit overwhelming, that one would be best. So, he stayed outside in case we needed anything."

"Oh."

Your family loves you, Legs. They'll do anything for you. I'd do anything for you.

But you can't die for me, I replied to Auwei, *they can. And I don't want that. But there will be other missions... and I'll have to put these people I love so dearly in harm's way. Some of them may die, and that will definitely be my fault. How can I do that? How can I send them out? How can I live with that?*

I don't know, Legs. Perhaps talk to Crane. Maverick must have dealt with feelings like this too. Perhaps she knows how he dealt with it.

He was a rock. I...

I'd been about to say I can't imagine him suffering over the deaths of others... but instantly I knew that was wrong. He'd cared deeply for everyone in his House. Just because I'd never seen him suffering, didn't mean it didn't happen.

Perhaps you're right.

"Sparrow, can you fetch Crane for me? I'd like to talk to her."

"Of course, my love." She kissed the top of my head, then extricated herself from under me.

I sat up on my bed as she left.

Silence returned with food as Sparrow returned with Crane.

I ate from the plate of cold meats and soft breads, hard cheese and dried fruit. Crane sat in the hard chair at the small table in my room and waited patiently.

"We'll be just outside," Sparrow said and exited, shooing out Silence.

"You want to talk about failed missions?" Crane asked. "About the people in your House who'll die? About... all the pressures you're feeling. Am I right?"

I nodded. "Are you sure your spirit-gift isn't mind-reading."

She smiled softly. "No, but I've been through this before."

"With Maverick?"

"Yes."

"I can't picture him crying in his room," I murmured. "Even though I know he cared deeply for all of us."

"He did. And he did cry... sometimes. More often he'd turn into a bull and go ruin a few fences out in our farmers' fields." The side of her mouth quirked into a sad smile. A tear passed over her cheek. "But you're right, he wouldn't let it show. I was the only one who knew. Our House budget went to mending a lot of fences."

I let out a hoarse laugh at that, before sniffing back a few tears of my own. "So... what do I do?"

Crane's sad smile shifted as her face fell a little. She sighed. "That I can't really answer. You'll know how best to grieve and deal with loss, but I think there are a few things you need to know which may help... or may not, I don't know."

That seemed ambiguous. I raised a brow in question.

"First... know that, if we disagree with one of your plans, if we think it's too dangerous or too... something, whatever, we'll let you know. We all agreed that as crazy as this plan to kidnap the queen was, it was the best plan. And to be fair, it worked. Everything we planned for worked. We just weren't prepared for the queen herself being cursed. No one could have known that. You can't blame yourself." She sighed. "Well, you can, but it wasn't you who killed her. It was the mistweaver who cursed her."

I nodded to that. I still blamed myself, but her words made sense.

"So yes, some of us might die, but it will never be just your call if that happens. We will all agree on the plan and go willingly, knowing the dangers."

"Did knowing that help Maverick?"

"Ah... well... no."

"That's what I thought. Go on." I nibbled on some cheese as she continued her list of *things I should know*.

"Second, we know that you're willing to die for us."

I blinked at that, brow furrowing. I hadn't been expecting that. Was I willing to die for my House? The answer came quickly: yes, I was.

"And none of us want to lose you, just as you don't want to lose any of us."

Interesting. I hadn't thought of things in reverse. How others would feel if I died. I supposed they'd feel how I'd feel if *they* died.

"And *because* we don't want you to die, we'd die for you, Legs. We know, you'd die for us just as easily. It's a give and take. I know that doesn't make dealing with any of our deaths any easier, just as your death wouldn't be any easier for us. But you have to understand... we're all in this together. We'll all stand up for every other member of this House. And that means putting our lives on the line occasionally. Just as we know you'd put your life on the line for us."

It was certainly a different perspective. I nodded. "Thank you."

"Finally — and this is something that never came up with Maverick — we know that right now is a very difficult time for all of us." She gave a harsh little laugh. "Legs, we all know that what we're facing is next to impossible. We're a small house, ten people, going up against the entirety of the rest of our nation. That's... madness, but we're doing it because it's right, because we know it needs to be done. And we're doing it because we know *you* can do it."

"Can I?" I asked, voice quiet. I put my plate aside and gazed hard at Crane. "Do you really think that?"

She stared back just as hard. Her voice didn't waver

when she said: "I do." She gave a grim smile. "Because our enemies have already foreseen it. They know you'll defeat them and it scares The Pits out of them!"

Oh... right.

"What's more," she added, "I don't think Maverick could have done it."

I raised a brow at that. "Truly? I thought he could do anything!"

"Almost anything, perhaps, but he tackled problems head on. He knew tactics and strategies, but often ignored the devious way of doing things in favor of the direct. And this isn't a problem we can attack head on. But you, Legs, you think in all manner of weird and wonderful ways. And it's that kind of thinking that's going to get us through this. I know we have the help of Alvere and Vauphan, but I also know they won't be able to divert many resources to help us. Your plan to use the Fey on the mission to get the queen was inspired."

"That was Alvere's idea, not mine."

"But you picked it up and ran with it, making it work." Crane rose and came to sit on the bed next to me, she took up one of my hands and held it gently between both of hers. "Legs, the world has turned to madness and we're the only ones who know it. We all know that it might mean our deaths to do this, but we all believe that you are our best chance of getting through this alive."

That was something I was still curious about. I shook my head, brow furrowed. "Why?" I asked, perhaps a bit too harshly. "You all made me your leader, but... why? Why do you think I can do this? Just because I don't think in a straightforward way? That can't be it." Even before she could answer I rushed on. "I'm the second youngest member of the House, others have more experience or are stronger, others are more conniving or devious, I'm sure. Why me?"

She squeezed my hand. "You're right, of course," she began softly. "Others are more devious, or stronger, or experienced, but..." She paused and made sure she had my gaze upon hers before she went on, holding me in suspense. "None of them have all of those qualities in as great a quantity as you do, Legs." She smiled. "Your spirit-gift is bloody *Heroism* for Pit's sake!" I'd never heard Crane swear like that, twice in one sentence.

I blinked, still not quite understanding.

She went on. "Legs, you may not be as strong as Ant, or as curious and odd as Foggy, or as experienced as Midnight, but you're more of all of those qualities combined than any of those others.

"Even Midnight?" I asked, a bit disbelieving. "She's pretty bloody strong and experienced and—"

"And her spirit-gift is going unseen, Legs. Don't you see? What leader can lead from the shadows? She knows that. You're out there, first into the fray and fighting just as hard as anyone else. So yes, she might be stronger and more experienced, but she doesn't have the one other quality that makes a good leader: the will to lead." Crane smiled once again. "Legs... she's terrified of leading. If you think you're scared, she's ten times as worried as you are. Why do you think she never even became a squad leader? She hates giving orders. She doesn't want to be in charge of people. She works best alone and she knows it."

"Oh." I hadn't known any of that. "Everyone really sees me that way? As a leader?" I tried to think of what I'd done to inspire such thoughts.

"You should hear Silence tell the story of how you saved him from the mistweaver, valiantly fighting the impossible foe yourself, keeping her at bay so he could get away with the information from the Vauphani raid."

I suppose I had done that.

"More than that," she whispered softly. "People... love you, Legs. Even more than those you share your bed with. There is just something about you that draws people to you. We all feel it."

"You're not interested in sharing my bed, are you?" I wasn't attracted to Crane. I saw her more as a mother figure.

She laughed. "No, Legs, I'm not. And I believe not everyone will be, but still... you're just... easy to know. You're open about how you feel and people are drawn to that sort of openness I think." She smiled. "*That* was something Maverick didn't do well. He kept his feelings hidden for the most part. People were still drawn to him, but more... as a curiosity, I think. They wanted to know more about him because he was so closed off." She shrugged. "I don't know if that's it or not, but I know people love you, Legs."

"Oh."

"And don't worry, the ones who aren't in your little harem don't feel left out. From what I've seen, Princess and Foggy are becoming quite close." She cocked her head to one side. "And I could be wrong, but there's been something in how your sister has been looking at Fin."

That surprised me. "Truly?"

She shrugged. "Perhaps it's nothing."

"And for you?" I asked.

"Alas, I've always pined for people I couldn't have." I did notice how she didn't say men. "And I'm an old woman now. I fear there won't be anyone for me."

"You're not that old." I figured her to be in her forties, no older.

She smiled. "I hope you're right."

Some strange little part of me made it my mission to find someone for Crane... and Midnight... if they wanted someone. After this whole war thing was done, I'd focus on that.

For now... I had other things to worry about.

And something Crane had said had gotten me thinking. "We need help," I stated.

"Yes," she said.

I pulled my hand out from hers as I smiled and rose, ready to get back to work. "And I think I know where to get it."

CHAPTER 8

SILENCE

SILENCE SQUIRMED. HE WANTED TO HELP, KNEW HE COULD help, but he didn't like this plan at all. Even though he had volunteered for this mission.

Legs' plan was to talk to Blackclaw. Hopefully their old friend wouldn't think Legs was a horrible traitor. Then Blackclaw would convince Grizzly House of that same fact. As soon as he'd heard Blackclaw's name, Silence knew he had to come along. He hadn't known exactly how he could help, but he was the only other person who knew Blackclaw well, so him making contact made sense.

He just hadn't known how to do that. He'd had the entirety of the trip to Cragmount to think but hadn't come up with anything.

Fin hadn't been able to take them. The Grizzly House Manor — Stonehold — was in the badlands in the north-west of Elista. Since Fin had never been inland in the west, the closest he could get the team was to a small coastal village in the southwest of Elista called Bell Cove.

There had been some debate over who would go. Silence had made his case, Midnight would come for her stealth, Fin for his transport — even if he couldn't get them in quick, he could get them out quick — and finally Ant as muscle if needed.

It had taken them a little more than two weeks to travel by carriage from that small coastal village to the town of Cragmount in the north. The ride hadn't been comfortable. Fin and Ant in the same carriage left little room for others, and since Fin's other form wasn't smaller, he remained as he was, while Silence and the others took turns in their avatar forms.

Once at Cragmount, Midnight procured the team two rooms at an inn, one with two beds for sleeping in shifts, the other for meeting and planning.

After one day of scouting, mostly by Midnight, they'd discovered that Blackclaw was at Stonehold and wasn't part of the Grizzly forces that had been sent east to help with the "war" with Vauphan.

And now, it was Silence's turn. He was the one going in... but he didn't like any of his options.

"I know, I know!" he said, holding up his hands to stall any more comments from the others. Fin was sleeping, as was Midnight. Ant and Legs were both staring him down. "I know I'm the best choice to go in and I know why... I just don't know how!" He squared his shoulders and straightened to his full height, which was just ever-so-slightly taller than Legs. "I can't walk up to their front door like this." He motioned to himself. "Which means I'd have to go in as a mouse, and there are a lot of things in that house — some of the avatars of the Nobles included — that would love to eat me."

He'd seen Stonehold from a distance, up on a higher hill than the aptly named Cragmount. This whole area was badlands, craggy, rocky hills, best for grazing sheep and mining the many minerals beneath the ground. Stonehold was a fortress and probably had any number of holes through which a mouse might sneak in. However, those dark places within the walls housed other denizens, many of which preyed on mice. And it wasn't a small fortress either. He'd have to go quite a long way as a small creature to reach Blackclaw's rooms.

Legs sighed. "I know you're scared, we're all—"

"I'm not scared!" he said, and instantly realized he sounded like a frightened child saying he wasn't scared. He calmed himself. "What I mean is. I'm not scared of dying for our cause or doing something dangerous... but... I may be just a bit scared of dying for no reason other than I was a tasty morsel. And if I do, you'll never even know what happened to me!" He sighed. "That seems... just so... sad."

"You want me to go with you?" Ant asked. "My avatar's even smaller."

Silence grimaced. "Then we'd both get eaten, a main course and dessert."

Legs laughed her unique I'm-thinking-something-dirty laugh then coughed and was serious again. "You've convinced me. We'll all go. My venom should stop most things in those walls. I'll make sure you get where you're going, and Ant and I will be there, just in case."

Silence nodded. It was settled.

They waited a full day to make sure they were rested then snuck out of the town and up to the manor in the darkness before dawn. They did indeed find a nice hole to slip in through and made their way up inside the walls of the ancient fortress.

As predicted, there were many interesting creatures living in those old walls, though the only one they found which posed any real threat, was a large rat, which Legs paralyzed. Silence felt a bit ashamed of his fear after that.

They made it to Blackclaw's rooms and found a small hole in the stone of the windowsill where the wooden frame had been worn away by rot over many years. Silence managed to squeeze through; the other two made it through the tiny hole easily.

Silence stayed on the sill for a moment taking in the room. There was a door in the far wall, probably leading to the rest of the keep. Not far from that, on the same wall, was a small nightstand, then a large bed. On the other side of the bed was an open area with a couple of chairs before a large hearth. In the close right-hand corner was a built-out area of wooden walls with a door. Probably a small privy. On the left-hand wall were a large wardrobe and a tall chest of drawers. The room was empty.

Silence waited for a while, just to make sure Blackclaw wasn't in the privy. Then he scampered down the wall and was halfway across the room when the door to the hall opened. He rushed under the bed, out of sight, and watched as two booted feet stepped into the room. He heard a heavy sigh. It sounded like Blackclaw was frustrated or perhaps tired?

She moved around the bed to the fireplace and threw some more wood on the embers of the fire, waiting for it to catch. It was spring, but this high up, in this drafty castle, it was chilly. She moved to one of the chairs before the fire and sat heavily with another sigh.

He ran out from under the bed on the far side before returning to himself, crouching low behind the large piece of furniture.

He drew in a long breath to steady himself, then rose.

"Hello Blackclaw, it's me, Silence, don't be afraid. I'm —" His words cut off as he caught site of her. She'd shot to her feet upon hearing his voice. She'd changed a lot in the nearly a year since he'd seen her last. Gone was the bulk from her figure, but remaining were all her curves. She was a stunning woman now, not slender, but fit and strong and much fuller of figure than Legs or Sparrow. Her black hair had been cut short, framing a narrower face, which seemed to enhance and enlarge her brown eyes.

She had claws out on her hands, but quickly put them away. "Silence?" She blinked. "What are you doing here?"

"I... ah..." He blinked his confused-attraction away. He had a group he loved very much, and who loved him. "I've come to ask for your help."

It was only then that she stiffened and her claws returned. "No, wait, you're... with the traitor." She looked around quickly. "Is she here?"

Silence held out his empty hands. "Please, Blackclaw, I'm here in peace. Don't call out, don't be alarmed. I just want to talk. Please?" He inched a bit closer to her, moving around to the end of the bed.

She settled again with a sigh, and he noticed then the darkness under her eyes, the fatigue upon her. "What am I doing?" she muttered to herself. Her claws vanished again, and she rushed to him, hugging him. "It's so good to see you." Her words were soft and low, but her hug was tight and strong, perhaps just a little too strong, too desperate.

Her ample body, pressed to his, distracted him, but he

quelled his startled arousal and returned her embrace. "It's good to see you too. Can we talk?"

She drew back and nodded. "Of course, come, sit." She motioned to the chairs, and they sat before the fire. Even before he began, she spoke, and the words came out in a rambling mess. "Spirits, Silence, what's been happening? I've heard so many things. I don't want them to be true, but, with the war and... she killed the queen for Spirits' sake! I... I don't know what to believe anymore. Are you here to flee from Legs? Has she harmed you? We'll take you in, I'm sure. I... Spirits, what am I saying? I don't even know. I'm sorry, what did you need to say? Why are you here?"

He smiled softly. "It may be a long story. Is there any chance we'll be interrupted?"

She shook her head. "No, I... well... ah... oh..."

"What is it?" Silence noted the flush of her cheeks.

She rose and went to the door, sliding a bolt to hold it closed. "I have a... friend who might stop by."

Silence had the distinct impression this *friend* was the sort that joins you in bed, given how flushed she'd become.

"She sometimes stops by in the afternoons if she's free. I'll tell her I'm not feeling well if she does." Blackclaw returned to her chair. "Go on."

Silence gathered his thoughts, then began with a measured pace. "What you've been hearing are just rumors, they are unfounded and mostly lies." He sighed. "The trouble is that they are coming from high up, so other Nobles tend to believe them. If you'll let me, I'd like to tell you a story. It... may be a bit hard to believe from your perspective, but I hope you'll keep an open mind."

She nodded, so he went on, telling her everything he and Legs and the once Maverick House had been through. He didn't quite tell it in order, jumping around a bit to add in the pieces he and his House had learned later, but which were earlier parts of this story. "And, she didn't kill the queen, though, the queen *is* dead. Whitewing had a mistweaver's curse upon her, and when she was taken from the capital, it was enacted. That is what killed her, not Legs. We were only trying to find out more of this plot and who was behind it. So no, I'm not here to flee from her or join with you. We're here to get your help, to try to convince you and your House that we're not evil, because we need help to take out those who are."

He could see the skepticism written clearly on Blackclaw's face. She'd listened without comment to his entire story, but now sighed. "Mistweavers?" It was clear she didn't believe in such things. "Silence, do you know how crazy that sounds?" She looked away into the now-dwindling flames of the fire. "But then... all of this is hard to believe." She shook her head. "But the Royal House being behind everything?" A grimace twisted her face. "Your story is just as outrageous as theirs. You're casting them as evil, while they do the same to you. How... how can I trust you... or them?" She threw her arms into the air and rose, pacing the room. "Spirits, what a mess." Then she stopped suddenly. She turned to him slowly. "You swear by the Spirits your story is true?" she asked slowly and there was something about how she asked, which made him shiver.

"Yes," he said with a confident nod.

"Then... there may be a way to convince not only me, but this entire house of that truth and get us on your side." She looked at the door to the hall for a long moment. "Will you come with me?" she ventured, tentative. "My *friend*... has a spirit-gift. She can determine the truth of anything. If you tell her your story...?" Yet Blackclaw seemed hesitant. She looked back to Silence. "Are you sure you want to do this?"

He nodded again, rising.

"Take me to her," he said with confidence.

"No," Legs said, appearing on the other side of Black-claw, leaning against the wall. She must have been listening in. "Take *me* to her."

CHAPTER 9

BLACKCLAW NEARLY JUMPED OUT OF HER SKIN, SPINNING WITH her claws out and ready. Then she saw me, saw I was relaxed and unarmed, and she settled, claws vanishing.

"Legs?" She laughed. "I should have known you'd not be far away." She hesitated only for a moment before coming to embrace me. I returned the gesture. She had certainly become quite the beautiful woman, though it seemed her time here had worn heavily upon her.

"I don't want any of this to be true," she whispered. "But I'd rather know the truth than keep believing a lie."

"I know," I said and we drew apart. "So, let's see this friend of yours."

Blackclaw nodded. "Just to be safe, both of you better return to your avatar forms, I'll carry you to her unseen."

Silence and I did as instructed and were put in a pouch, the draw-string pulled not completely closed so we'd have an escape if needed.

Then we trusted ourselves to the care of this old friend, not knowing where we were going, feeling only the jostling of the pouch at her hip. We heard a bit of muffled discussion then the bag was carefully being moved and opened. Silence and I clambered out and returned to our human forms.

We were in a larger room and Blackclaw's "friend" turned out to be Ursa, the second of House Grizzly. I didn't know all the members, but I knew her; she was hard to miss. One of the few women taller than me, over six feet of powerful physique, with cropped blond hair and stunning, deep blue eyes.

She started when she saw me... just as I was shocked to see her.

"They are my friends," Blackclaw said quickly. "Please don't hurt them. Just... listen with your gift, and we'll all know what the truth is."

Ursa calmed quickly, though I felt the latent power in those strong limbs. She was a full-figured woman like Blackclaw, just a little bigger and taller in all aspects. Strong and powerful and beautiful. She nodded. "I'll listen." But there was a threat in her voice. It was clear she didn't expect to believe our story.

We were in a sitting room, heavy carpets over the cold stone floor, and comfortable chairs surrounding a low table. A low fire burned in a nearby hearth but gave little heat. I paced to keep warm.

Ursa sat in a large chair and watched us keenly. She didn't seem to mind the cold.

Blackclaw nodded for me to begin, and I told them my tale.

The way Ursa twitched her nose from time to time made me believe she wasn't so much reading my mind as... smelling the truth of my words on me. Perhaps it was both?

Either way, when I finished, she looked a bit stunned, shaking her head slowly. "I can't believe it," she said slowly. "But I *must* believe it. Not a word of it was a lie. Still... how could our own Royal family be betraying us like this?"

Only then did I relax. I saw Blackclaw do the same, finally knowing we weren't lying to her.

Ursa looked at me for a long moment. "I need to take this to Grizzly. And I'll need to do some internal house-cleaning to see if we have any traitors working for the Royals in our midst. That will take some time, but we are with you, Legs of House Spider. Anything you need that we can provide we will."

"Can you recall your troops from the front?" I asked quickly.

Ursa frowned. "No. That would let the Royals know we were against them instantly. Perhaps it would be best if we played along for a bit to see what we can find out. But I'll let the commanders of our troops know they are not to fight or support those at the front in any way. We don't want to make things worse."

She sighed heavily. "How could we have come to this?" Shaking her head, she asked, "And you have no idea why the Royals are doing all of this?"

"That piece of the puzzle has eluded us. We do know they've been killing Nobles and their Lumani — somehow — because they knew too much. So, be very careful in how you move."

Ursa nodded to that. "It will take us a bit of time to get our house in order. How can we contact you?"

"Send a pigeon for mundane things, but they can be intercepted, so... for most things, we have a member of our House, Fin, who will come and go regularly to keep you up to date on events and carry messages back and forth. We'll need to bring him up from the village to someplace safe in your keep so he knows where to transport himself. That's his spirit-gift."

"Very useful."

"So is yours."

Ursa smiled. "Indeed." But her grin quickly faded. "It would be best if you were not seen here. We'll arrange to have your Fin brought up, but otherwise, you should go for now. I am not certain of everyone in my house yet. Some of the newer members from Blackclaw's cohort, have always been a bit... odd. I wouldn't want to give anything away." She sighed. "I do not like using my gift on members of my own House. I like to think I can trust them, but now... I will do what I must."

I nodded to that.

We were bundled into Blackclaw's pouch again and carried back to her room. It was only once we were there, and the door latched shut, that we returned to ourselves and spoke freely with Blackclaw.

We summoned Ant out from the hole in the wall, and Blackclaw tried not to drool over him, though I could see the instant attraction in her eyes. He remained to one side, while the three of us sat on her large bed and caught up.

"So..." I asked after enough other talk that I thought it safe. "You and Ursa are... together?" I smiled. "I'm happy for you. She seems like a wonderful woman."

Blackclaw blushed. "Yes, but... that's not the entire truth."

"Oh? Do tell," I said, leaning forward intently.

Her blush deepened. "I, ah... well, I worked very hard when I got here, trained relentlessly, and I began to lose a little weight and..." She laughed. "I never thought I'd catch anyone's eye, but—"

"I always thought you were beautiful," Silence admitted, no hint of hesitation in his voice.

She blushed. "I know, but... I... didn't really allow myself to believe it, I guess." She sighed. "Anyway, it wasn't just Ursa's eye I caught. You see, she and Grizzly have been together for some time and... they wanted me to join... *them*." She went from a blushing red, to a deep maroon, lips pressed tight for a moment.

Yet I only smiled. "Sounds lovely to me."

She blinked. "Oh?"

I reached out to touch her shoulder. "Yes. Perhaps I should mention — since I didn't talk much about my personal life during my retelling of the past year — that I'm now with a whole group of people."

"Oh?" Her eyes grew a little wide. She looked back and forth from me to Silence to Ant.

"Yes. Silence and I have been together, so have Ant and I. I'm also seeing Sparrow, a woman from my House, and... ah... the Prince — no, I guess he's King now — of Vauphan."

Blackclaw's jaw dropped. "Truly? A prince? And... all at once, or...?"

I took a bit of time to explain how the odd relationship worked, how we all loved each other... except for Ant, he'd only been with me so far, but... who knew what might happen. "And I'd be open to others if they were agreeable to the whole situation," I said with a grin.

Blackclaw looked a little stunned, then her eyes went a little wider. "Oh... wait, you don't mean... me? Do you?"

I laughed. "I wasn't thinking of you, no, but now that you mention it, you'd be welcome." I slid Silence a sidelong look. "I think Silence wouldn't mind warming your bed sometime."

I caught their combined blush at that. "I... ah.... appreciate the offer," she said... and I waited, but she didn't go on to explicitly deny it. Interesting.

We talked for the rest of the afternoon until it began to get dark. Then Ant, Silence, and myself took our avatar forms and crawled away through the walls. We didn't get back to the inn until well after dark. Midnight had food waiting, which we were all thankful for, not having eaten since breakfast.

"How did it go?" Midnight asked.

"We have an ally," I said between bites of warm bread and hearty stew. "Finally, things are starting to turn our way."

Now I just had to figure out what I was going to do with this newfound help.

CHAPTER 10

Alvere

Alvere stood just inside the cave, watching the tide slowly recede off the rocky beach before him. Somewhere, out across the expanse of Dyren's Bay was his home. Odd though, how he felt just as home here as he did there. In fact, he felt more at home here, amidst friends and lovers, not subjects and people who depended on him. Here he could be himself, there... he was *King* Alvere.

It would be known soon. With things calming in the North, he'd sent word that it would be well to do away with the charade of his cousin, Pierre being crowned. The country could know its true leader and true king had survived and would be leading them. But that also meant, his time here would be limited.

This vacation, away from his responsibilities, would soon end. He'd be a king in truth and have far too much on his plate to go galivanting off to see these dear people whom he loved. He'd grown close to all of them. With Legs and

Silence away, he'd spent time with Sparrow, gotten to know her better. They'd slept next to each other a couple of times, but only that, lying together for comfort and warmth in these chilly stone halls. They loved each other, but knew their hearts were given to another, the same other. It was Legs who truly made this group... work.

His half-Fey heritage did give him rather good hearing, and he caught the sounds of someone's footfalls crunching on the stones behind him, coming out from deep within the cave, where a rope ladder had been lowered down a long shaft, the "back door" of the house in the cliffs above.

Arms wrapped around him and warm soft lips kissed the back of his neck. "Hello my king," Legs whispered. "I'm back."

"How did it go?" he asked, putting his hands on her arms crossed over his stomach as he savored the feel of her lithe body pressed against his back.

"Very well. Grizzly House is on board." She sighed and slumped a little. "Now... I have no clue what to do." Another soft kiss on his neck. "I was hoping you might join me... join us... for some... inspiration?"

He smiled. "There is nothing I'd want more." He turned in her arms and swept her up in a passionate kiss, his heart thundering now that he held her, his home, his heart, his core. He curled a hand up into the waves of her brown hair, pressing her lips close, as his other hand found the small of her back and urged their bodies together. She slid a leg up his thigh, which pulled her skirt back to her hip. He ran a hand along that exposed skin as his arousal surged. His cock was hard and ready, yearning to be inside her. For just a moment, he wanted to be alone with her, selfish, wanting her just for him, not sharing... so he reveled in this passionate embrace for as long as she'd allow.

Finally, she drew back. Breathless, she said, "That was an excellent start. Shall we reconvene with the others?"

He nodded. He knew he had to share her... and he loved the others as well, if not... quite as much as he loved her. He smiled as he let his soul sink into those russet brown eyes. "Yes, lets."

She took his hand and led him back into the cave and to the ladder. They climbed up — it was a not-insignificant drop — and found the ledge and entrance back into the cliff-house. He could sense her excitement as she nearly dragged him to her room.

Inside, he was surprised to see Ant standing off to one side. The large man looked like he felt just a bit awkward and out of place. "He's just going to watch this time," Legs explained. "See what he likes."

If any more joined this already large group, things were going to start getting awkward quickly. Still Alvere smiled and nodded to Ant. "Glad to have you." The man was certainly much larger than anyone else in this group. It sent a shiver running down Alvere's spine to think of just how "large" Ant might be. Would he want such a massive erection inside him? From the sounds of Legs' encounter with the man, it was... painful but pleasurable.

He put those thoughts aside as his arousal grew. Legs was clearly eager, stripping off her clothes. Sparrow and Silence were already on the bed, mostly naked and gently caressing each other. He quickly disrobed as well, wishing to join them all.

Legs came to him and whispered in his ear, "Go get the oil from the bedstand, I want you inside me like you were with Silence last time."

Alvere's eye's widened in shock. "Truly?"

"Oh, yes. I know exactly what I want." She stepped back

and finished disrobing, and he took just a moment to marvel at her form: that perfect fall of brown hair, the soft wide lips, and those red-brown eyes. Some men might be put off by her strong shoulders and arms, not delicate and lady-like, but he loved every part of her. Her breasts were not large but full, ample pear-shaped swells with those small but sensitive nipples. Her waist and belly were taut and tight, her hips, curved but not rounded. It was her namesake legs, which truly sealed his desire for her, long and lean, allowing her to move so swiftly and gracefully as she mounted the bed and whispered to Sparrow and Silence.

They would all give her whatever she desired. She was their goddess, their truest love, their center. She didn't know it. She thought them all in this together, but in truth, they were all in this for her. Alvere had discussed it with Silence and Sparrow at varying times and they'd all agreed they'd not tell her. She wouldn't believe it. She was too humble to think she could be the center of so many people's worlds. So, they'd continue to love her and love each other and do whatever she asked of them. If it pleased her, they rejoiced in it.

Alvere got the oil from the drawer, noting Ant's awkward fumbling as he got out his oh-dear-gods massive shaft, stroking it slowly as he watched the naked bodies positioning themselves on the bed.

When he turned back to the bed, his arousal spiked. This was... new.

Silence lay on his back, and Sparrow was kneeling, hovering over his face. Alvere couldn't see, but he assumed Silence would be pleasuring the woman with his mouth. Sparrow faced Legs, who was currently straddling Silence's hips, still high, man-handling Silence's erection — and using her own fingers — on her folds to tease her arousal.

She leaned back a little on Silence's upraised legs as she slowly teased him into her, sinking down to straddle him, leaning forward to kiss Sparrow, forming a triangle of sorts with the three bodies. Silence then spread his legs, his thighs on top of Legs' calves behind her, and Legs looked to Alvere with longing in her eyes. "Your turn," she said, voice already hitching with rising bliss as she rocked herself on Silence.

Alvere took the hint, moving behind her. First, he doled out some oil onto his hands, liberally spreading it around Legs' rear opening, massaging the tight and puckered hole before inserting a finger to help massage the oil into her.

Legs gasped and moaned, even with just Alvere's finger inside her. Though, in truth she was also fully enjoying Silence's erection, not to mention Sparrow's hands on her breasts and lips on her mouth. Just seeing her passion mount, her pleasure rise, was nearly too much for Alvere. His urgency grew as he oiled her more, slipping another finger inside her, then a third, working them around until she began to loosen. He hoped she was ready. He was more than ready himself, and he knew she'd be tight and the pressure upon him exquisitely hard and needful.

He couldn't wait any longer and moved in closer, liberally oiling himself before pushing the flared tip of his erection into her.

"Oh, Spirits!" she cried out, going still, then shuddering, a tremble which seemed to run from her head to her toes, then back. "Oh, yes, more," she gasped, clearly already quite over-taken with ecstasy.

He grabbed her hips and thrust himself fully inside her in one hard plunge, and she stiffened again. "Oh, Spirits, it's... oh!" She was having trouble speaking, so Sparrow stopped her lips with a kiss. Alvere, Silence, and Sparrow all threw themselves into pleasuring this amazing woman.

As Alvere had expected she was so very tight, clamping down upon him with delicious intensity. It was only the oil which allowed him to continue to thrust into her. Despite his earlier urgency and the pressure squeezing him, he found himself not finishing as quickly as he'd expected. He wanted this to last for Legs, and it seemed he was able to delay his gratification, riding his own pleasure, building and building, intensifying and focusing until he was as engorged and ready as he'd ever been, but still holding his release.

Legs was gasping, murmuring words as she shook through the throes of, what seemed like, one prolonged orgasm. She leaned back against Alvere, and he held her, moving his hands up to her breasts, cupping them, holding and caressing them, feeling their weight and the tight towers of her nipples. He flicked one of those nubs and she seemed to half-collapse with another surge of bliss. Over her shoulder he saw Sparrow, clasping her own small breasts, eyes clenched shut as Silence brought her to release.

Alvere heard Silence's grunt and saw the man's hands grasp Legs thigh's tighter as he bucked up from under them in a final thrust. Alvere slid one of his hands down Legs' sweaty body to her opening, feeling the pulse of Silence's erection as the other man came. Then Alvere slowly circled Legs' clit.

She trembled and gasped.

He flicked that sensitive nub, then began rubbing it furiously.

"Oh, Spirits! Yes!" Legs cried out and she clamped down hard upon him, shuddering through a powerful release. With that Alvere allowed himself to join the others in a jolting, body-shaking mutual orgasm, holding Legs tight to him, feeling her body thrum in time with his as they came together.

Legs leaned her head back on his shoulder and they kissed, if a bit awkwardly, before her gaze caught on something and she sat up a little.

"What did you think?" she said to Ant, her breath still catching as she shuddered with the aftershocks of their joining.

Alvere turned his head and saw Ant, stroking a raging erection, with a look of semi-pained restraint on his face.

"Want to join us?" Legs asked him.

He nodded quickly, no words. He moved to the bed as everyone else slowly disengaged from each other. Legs slid off the bed, and sank down before Ant. "Let's give you a little release first, yes?" she said as she grasped his erection and moved it into her mouth. With his size, she couldn't take much of him, but it didn't seem like that would be needed. Almost as soon as he was in her mouth he grunted, his shaft twitching as he came.

Alvere wondered what it would be like to have a man that large in *his* mouth. The thought aroused him far more than he'd expected. He'd have never thought to be with a man before he met Legs, but with her, anything and everything was possible; not just possible, but arousing and exciting and enticing.

Once Ant was spent, Legs remained where she was, bringing him back to arousal with her mouth. Alvere caught movement from the corner of his eye to see Sparrow doing the same with Silence. And once the other man was ready, Sparrow turned to Alvere with a questioning glance. He shook his head, watching these two women arouse these two men had him almost fully engorged once again.

Though, now with the extra member in their group he had no clue how they'd come together.

It was Ant who initiated the next position. Once he was ready, he told Legs, "Enough!" and she rose. He laid her back on the bed, kneeling at the side, between her legs, heartily pleasuring her with mouth and hands. Legs then reached out toward Silence and Alvere's erections. They moved to either side of her so she could stroke the two of them, moving her head from side to side to take them into her mouth in turn.

Sparrow moved over Legs, giving Ant a second set of folds to pleasure with hands and lips. She alternated between kissing Legs and taking Silence and Alvere in her mouth as well. Those two sets of lips and grasping hands were quickly bringing Alvere to a peak of arousal, just as Ant's earnest ministrations were making both women moan with pleasure.

Ant rose partially, erection in hand, moving it back and forth between the two sets of wet folds, teasing and testing.

"Too big for me," Sparrow breathed, and shifted off Legs. Ant then focused his attentions on Legs, slowly working his massiveness into her. They began a tentative rhythm which forced the others away. Legs focused entirely on Ant.

Legs wrapped her legs around Ant and drew herself up to cling to him as he supported her with his hands under her thighs. He stood, holding her easily in his arms as he rocked his hips to push that huge erection into her, then pull it out in slow thrusts.

The remaining three on the bed were distracted, watching Ant's massive length slowly pushing in then pulling out of Legs.

Silence moved behind Sparrow, his hands on her body, working her to another shuddering release.

Alvere was left a little uncertain, until Ant seemed to sense his desires.

Ant knelt at the side of the bed, spreading his legs out to lower him and Legs to the right level. Alvere didn't need quite as much oil to get her rear opening ready again and was soon inside her. The feel of her pulsing canal gripping him — and the shifting of Ant's erection inside her as well — surged his bliss to a sublime instance of purest pleasure.

Legs was already in her murmuring-incoherent-words-while-trembling stage of mid-orgasmic bliss and Ant had his eyes rolled back, breathing through his teeth, clearly ready to release, but holding himself from it. Alvere himself maintained long, slow strokes, feeling his own release building, the exquisite intensity of pressure swelling his erection to near painful extremes as he too waited for just the moment...

Then Legs convulsed with a powerful orgasm, clamping down upon him and he could hold it no longer. He joined with the other two in a massive release. Something clicked into place in Alvere's soul as he shivered through that epitome of bliss, tears of ecstatic joy and fulfillment on his cheeks.

He may be a king, but this was where he belonged, giving everything he had to the woman he loved.

It took a long time for them to finish their chain of pleasure before staggering apart. They fell to the floor or the bed, weak and smiling, like this had been their first time.

Legs laughed, a thing of purest joy and relief. "Spirits Above and Below!" she breathed. "That was amazing. I'm ready to take on the world!"

Alvere smiled. That was what he — what they all — had been hoping for.

CHAPTER 11

"Okay, so, what do we know so far?" I asked, once again pacing the front of the common area. "The queen didn't give us any information, unfortunately, other than Merlin is... something, perhaps the mastermind behind all of this? But we don't know that for certain. So, let's start from the beginning, what do we know?"

Crane began the brainstorming session: "Some Nobles are seizing lands in the North, why, we're not quite sure, but even most of the Nobles in the northern army don't seem to know why either."

"Lynx said it was something about the Mists?" I recalled that from my conversation with him, before he'd been told I was a traitor, when he'd still been a friend. "He said that they were told Vauphan wanted to invade and claim the lands with the Mists."

"Which we don't, just to be clear," Alvere said.

"I know," I said with a smile, rolling my eyes. "They were told they needed to claim the northern provinces of Vauphan preemptively to stop the invasion, which makes little sense to me, but apparently made sense to them."

"Or perhaps it didn't make sense," Silence suggested. "Didn't Lynx also say something about those who questioned the orders were the ones who vanished?"

"Yes." I nodded. "That's right. So maybe it didn't make sense to them either, but it was do or disappear. That's an interesting thought." I pondered that for a moment. "I can't imagine Jaguar wasn't in on it though, either that or he was just extremely loyal to the nation and wasn't questioning things, which seems a bit... well... extreme." And we'd not be able to ask him now. He was dead, Ant's revenge for killing Amber. "So, three years ago, they invade Vauphan and anyone who seems overly concerned or questioned this... disappeared, which meant everyone remaining went along with it, whether it made sense or not," I summed up. "And we still don't know why."

"Yeah," Ant drawled. "That excuse about the Mists seems a bit flimsy to me."

I agreed.

Crane said, "And we know Merlin, Hale, and Horn are in on it." It was a testament to how disgusted she must be with them to not say their titles.

"Perhaps Lady Swan," I added, having seen her on Hale's arm. "But that's less certain."

"And it has to be more than just them for all of this to be kept hidden and to disappear those in the north who needed disappearing," Foggy said. "I can believe some people followed them just because they were important, but... disappearing someone... that would require some extreme loyalty or knowledge of what's going on."

"Which lends more credence to Jaguar being in on it." I finished that thought. "And yes, probably many others as well."

"But we don't know who," Princess added.

"We know we can trust Grizzly house though," Silence piped up.

I hated to disagree with him but... "Well, not yet."

That raised a few brows.

I wasn't sure we could trust Grizzly entirely, not yet. We could trust Blackclaw, but as for Ursa? We had proven ourselves to her... but she had done nothing to prove herself to us. It was something that had occurred to me when my mind had cleared after that mind-bending, body-breaking, world-shattering sex. I usually had my best ideas after sex.

It's all those wonderful chemicals surging through you, Auwei said analytically.

Among other things 'surging' inside me.

Do I have to scrub out that filthy mind of yours?

Oh, you know you love it.

Auwei giggled.

"Blackclaw we can trust," I stated. "But it occurred to me earlier that Ursa and the others haven't really done anything to prove they're on our side. They didn't kill us and they did listen to us... but that might be a long-con."

"But then Blackclaw might be in danger!" Silence said, worried.

"Yes, that occurred to me too. Unfortunately, we'll have to wait and see what happens with them. Either we can trust them or they'll betray us. We'll need to be ready for anything, until they've proven they're on our side, all of them."

Silence was still worried but nodded. "Perhaps..." He seemed to be thinking as he spoke. "We could ask for Blackclaw as a sort of liaison, keeping her here?"

That was an excellent idea, except... "We already have a liaison, pigeons and Fin. It would be odd to ask for her to stay with us... but I can try it, feel out their reactions."

Silence nodded. I'd do it for him, even if it did cause some questions on Grizzly's end of things.

"Perhaps," Crane began slowly. "Perhaps there is a way they can prove themselves, though it would be dangerous and potentially an opportunity for them to betray us as well."

"What are you thinking?" I asked, curious.

I felt Auwei's curiosity too.

Crane rose and began pacing, which was odd for her, usually so stoic and calm. "What if we use Grizzly as a way into the thick of things?" she asked, clearly a rhetorical question. "What if Ursa approaches Merlin and the others, saying she knows what's going on and wants in. With her ability to read minds or sniff out the truth, whatever it is, it wouldn't be out of the realm of reason for her to have gleaned the conspiratorial information off someone. So, she goes in and joins them. She could work on the inside for us, find out everything we need to know to prove these people are traitors." She stopped her pacing. "And perhaps she could even get some of us in close as well? That would be the risky part. If she *is* in on it, we'd be walking into a trap with her leading us along."

It was an interesting idea, and I agreed, potentially dangerous for Ursa and potentially very dangerous for us if we went in with her and she was a traitor. But we had to start somewhere. A plan began to form in my mind and a smile spread on my lips as I figured out exactly how we could make it work... and keep anyone who went in with Ursa as safe as possible.

CHAPTER 12

SPARROW

SPARROW WAS SCARED AND UNCOMFORTABLE, BUT SHE'D promised Legs she could do this, and she'd follow through, even if it meant she might die.

Ursa had agreed to their plan. She'd go in, supposedly alone, to join up with Merlin, Hale, and the others. The hope was to find out the true reason for all the machinations. Yet Ursa wouldn't be alone. The trouble was Hale's ability to revert any True-Bonded back to their original form. It meant hiding as an avatar wouldn't work, but there was something Hale couldn't affect.

Which was how Sparrow found herself in a strange dark place, hiding with Ahmaia, who'd used her cloth ability to hide them both in one of her 'pockets' which was in turn hidden inside a small pouch on Ursa's belt. Neither Sparrow nor Ahmaia would be able to see what was happening. Sparrow could only see a spot of light above her — the opening of the pouch — which seemed, at the same time, both close and incredibly distant.

Yet, they'd be able to hear events beyond the pouch to get a sense for how things progressed.

"We are in a large hall," Ahmaia said.

Sparrow could hear the echoing footfalls of Ursa as she moved into the chamber.

Then a deep, hard voice cut over the dying echoes of those footfalls. "Welcome Lady Ursa, it is our honor to have you here with us."

"Lord Hale, Lady Swan, Lady Merlin," Ursa said. "It is an honor to be here."

Sparrow silently thanked Lady Ursa. Now they knew who was in the hall with them.

"With the traitors of Maverick House having killed our beloved queen, I would ask that you address Merlin as My Queen or Your Majesty." This from Hale as well.

"Indeed, that news was horrible, I still can't quite believe it," Ursa said sounding shocked. "How did they do it?"

"Right in the very streets of this great city!" Hale said, voice raised in rage. "The used some fire magic to incinerate her where she stood! It was horrible to see."

Wow, that was — at the same time — so very far from the truth but vaguely believable.

"It must have been. I'm so sorry you had to witness that, and I'm sorry that we have all lost such a great woman." Ursa went on to say, "But surely, Lady Merlin, you will abide by the Council of Nobles when they meet to select a new Royal. They haven't selected you yet."

"They most certainly will." Hale's voice was low, lethal, threatening, but also with a hint of glee.

"Indeed," Ursa said, and nothing more on that topic.

Sparrow was just a bit shaken. The implication that the Council of Nobles would be so easily swayed to select Merlin was preposterous. There were many other more experienced leaders. Skyfire was the most likely candidate. Even Silvermane — the previous queen's daughter — had a shot at the throne.

A new voice joined the conversation. It was a powerful alto, a woman's voice, commanding and sure, but with just a hint of something Sparrow couldn't place, something just a little bit... off. "Check her for any True-Bonded avatars," the voice commanded.

"As you wish, My Queen," Hale said, indicating the previous speaker had been Merlin herself.

Heavy footfalls echoed in the chamber, growing louder, closer: Hale was coming.

This was the true test of how well Ahmaia's hidden pocket would work. They hadn't been sure if Hale could sense Lumani in addition to his other powers, but if so, and he sensed Sparrow and the presence of her Lumani: Ahena, this would all be over soon.

Sparrow's heart thundered in her chest. She clenched her eyes shut, not that it would do her any good in the event of discovery, but she needed to do something. She needed to be able to move some part of her, have some agency over what was happening, and shutting her eyes was virtually the only thing she could do.

"I recall Hale from the day of the queen's speech, a large and powerful man," Ahmaia said. "Does he scare you that much?"

Short answer: yes. Sparrow was well trained in a style of fighting which made her small size a strength, not a weakness, but she had never been comfortable in a true fight. She might be able to defeat Hale, she'd bested Ant a few times in her practices, but not every time, not by a longshot. If a large man could simply grapple her, pin her arms and keep her off the ground, all she could do then was flail her legs and hope to hit something vital. Also, with Hale's powers, she'd not be able to veer into her avatar form to escape.

Sparrow tried to calm her rapid breathing, taking long deep breaths before she replied. "I'll do what I must, if I must," she breathed; she couldn't help but keep her voice low. Ahmaia had said no one outside the pouch would hear them, but still...

Moments passed with no word or sound other than shuffling feet. Sparrow couldn't help but feel like any moment she'd be discovered and then...

"No, there are no other True-Bonded here," Hale said, almost sounding a bit disappointed. "They'd have reverted to their true form by now. She is alone."

Sparrow allowed herself to begin breathing normally again and was surprised to hear Ahmaia's sigh of relief accompanying her own.

They'd made it past the test.

"Come forward," Merlin said, cold and commanding.

There came several sets of echoing footfalls, the sounds mixing, making it hard to determine exactly who was moving.

"Hale follows closely behind us," Ahmaia said.

Sparrow nodded her thanks for that clarification.

"Why have you come?" Merlin said, suspicion plainly evident in the woman's voice.

Ursa responded, sure and confident. "I was concerned for those of my house going to the front. I wished to go myself and see what was happening there."

"Oh?" Merlin cut in quickly.

"Yes, My Queen, I took a fast carriage to the front." Ursa sighed heavily. "I was discouraged to hear of the loss of the

Nobles there. I surveyed the front and... I must admit I was surprised. What I saw did not match with what I'd been hearing about the war. Both sides are dug in and the Vauphan forces do not seem that extensive. So, I tracked down one of the few remaining Nobles of House Panther. He said the previous orders had come from Lord War himself, who'd been there recently, but was now missing. I... I just want to know more about what my men are walking into. Something doesn't feel right."

"You dare question the queen!" Hale's voice was vicious.

"Unhand me!" Ursa's voice was equally as hard. There was some movement, as the pouch bounced a little, and Sparrow could hear grunts, then a hard thump and gasp.

Ahmaia gave a low chuckle. "I think Ursa just put Hale in his place."

Good. Sparrow would have loved to have seen that.

"Hale, calm yourself. We should not assault our Nobles. Ursa, if you wouldn't mind releasing him?"

"Yes, My Queen." More rustling of clothes.

"Good."

For a moment no one spoke, but Sparrow could hear Hale rising, grunting, and moving away. A softer feminine voice then cooed over him quietly. Lady Swan no doubt.

"Tell me, Lady Ursa," Merlin began softly. That odd quality to her voice was back. "What is more important: maintaining Elista and her powers at all costs, or maintaining peace?"

Ursa took a long moment before answering: "Elista must remain strong, even if that means war."

"Good, I'm glad you agree."

Sparrow wondered how much of Ursa's responses were lies and what was truth. Legs hadn't been entirely sure they could trust Ursa, which was why it was only Sparrow on this mission with Ahmaia. If things went badly, she could try to fly away, and if that didn't work, at least it would be only her which was lost. She didn't like that option, but she'd agreed to do this for Legs; she'd do anything for Legs. The thought of the other woman, her truest love, sent a thrill through Sparrow. Thinking of Legs always made her smile, gave her strength and courage, and made her so desperately wish to be back in the arms of her lover. She pulled her mind away from that to listen. She needed to know if Ursa would betray them. She hadn't yet, but...

"And what do you think of the traitor Maverick and his House of filthy betrayers?" Merlin's voice rose just a little, not in volume, but intensity, that odd quality more pronounced now.

Ursa's reply was quick: "I do not know what happened with that once Noble House. I've heard that Maverick betrayed us and went over to Vauphan, and that his House is now in hiding. Obviously, they found a way to come here to the capital to kill the queen, which I cannot comprehend at all, but I do not know much more than that."

"And what does that tell you? What do you think of their actions?"

"They have betrayed us all."

"And...?"

"And for that, they should be hunted down and slain. And for the one who murdered the queen, the death should not be quick but torturous and slow."

Wow. Sparrow desperately hoped Ursa was just telling Merlin what she wished to hear. The other option was not pleasant to contemplate.

Merlin sighed. "I'm glad you agree, Lady Ursa." Something in Merlin's voice suggested she relaxed a little.

Ahmaia said, "Despite her words, I sense no duplicity

from Ursa, I do not think she will betray us." She reached out to touch Sparrow's shoulder, a strong and firm hold. "I have not sensed anything in her tone which would indicate she is doing anything other than playing along, telling Merlin what she wishes to hear. I think we will be well, little one."

Little one? Sparrow wasn't tall by any means, but Ahmaia was a half head shorter still. Though Ahmaia was probably something like two hundred years old — even though she looked Sparrow's age — or something like that; no one knew how long Fey actually lived.

"And tell me, Lady Ursa, will you do *anything* for Elista?" Merlin's tone became twisted, a hint of sadistic glee sneaking into it. Sparrow then realized what the odd quality to Merlin's voice had been and still was: the woman was insane. "If it was for the good of the entire country, would you kill some of our own citizens?"

"I... ah..." Sparrow could hear the moment's hesitation in Ursa's voice. Yet it quickly resolved. "Yes. Though I would never wish for the deaths of any Elistans. If it were necessary, for the greater good of Elista and must be done, then I would sorrow in the act, but I would do what was required."

"Do not sorrow to kill traitors, Ursa. Never that." Merlin seemed pleased. A long silence stretched after this. Sparrow wondered what was happening. It frustrated her to just listen, not able to do anything. Yet she was ever so curious what would come next.

"Come with me," Merlin said, and there was the rustle of fabric and soft footfalls. "Hale, you are dismissed." Then in a more confidential tone, closer and quieter: "We need to speak in private."

Two sets of footfalls padded along for some time before a door could be heard opening then closing.

"Sit," Merlin said. And again, fabrics shifted and the pouch jostled.

Sparrow hadn't known she was holding her breath until she had to let it out suddenly, starting to feel strained, struggling to breathe.

"Would you agree that the Mists are at the core of Elista's identity as a nation?" Merlin probed, voice manic.

"Yes," Ursa said quickly.

"And what if we no longer possessed the Mists?"

Ursa didn't answer right away. When she did, she spoke slowly, "You believe Vauphan will try to take them from us?"

Merlin chuckled. "No, that is only the tale we have told everyone else, the truth... is far more infuriating as there is little we can do about it."

Silence.

Merlin continued: "The truth is that the Mists are moving. In fact, they've always been moving, but so slowly we hadn't noticed it until recently. They shift perhaps a quarter of a mile a year, but they are shifting *toward* Vauphan, you see. They've always been close to our border, but in twenty years, they'll be on the border, and in a hundred years they'll be mostly in Vauphan. The Mists will no longer be ours... unless we conquer the north of Vauphan first."

Ursa released a heavy breath. "That's horrible. No wonder you've acted as you have. We must protect the Mists at all costs!"

"Indeed."

Sparrow understood. All of this, the deaths and war... were to protect the Mists. But... Sparrow knew Vauphan didn't want the Mists, didn't care about them. They probably would have been happy to have Elistans make the pilgrimage into their lands to visit them. And... that wouldn't be for a hundred years or more.

"What can I do to help?" Ursa asked, intent and sounding eager.

"I'm glad you ask." Merlin practically purred. "With your ability to seek out the truth, I have a special mission for you: seek out and find that bitch Legs and the remainder of Maverick House. Kill them, kill them all!" Merlin's voice had risen to a fanatical, maniacal, semi-laugh. "If you can do that, you can ask anything from me once I am crowned as the new queen, and it shall be granted."

"Thank you, My Queen. I see now why you must be queen. You are the only one who truly understands what's at stake."

"Yes, indeed. The others will understand and fall in line."

"I'm sure they will. And I will not fail you in this mission. I swear House Maverick shall be no more soon enough." Those words made Sparrow feel a chill... but then... perhaps Ursa's words were an inside joke. Maverick house was already gone. In its place was Spider House.

"Thank you, Lady Ursa, that is all. You may go."

"Thank you, My Queen."

Fabric shifted, feet scuffed, then came footfalls and the sound of a door opening and closing. Then only the single footfalls for some time before Ursa dared to speak again. "Well... that was informative," she whispered.

Yet still she walked for some time. Only once it sounded like she was in some private room, far away, did she say, "You can come out now."

Sparrow gasped as the world spun into light and largeness. She staggered, falling to the floor and sitting there for a long moment.

"Did you hear all of that?" Ursa asked in a whisper as she pulled closed the curtains over the one window in the room. They were back in the inn they'd stayed in the previous night.

"We did," Ahmaia responded before Sparrow was recovered enough to speak.

Ursa turned back to them. "She's completely mad." The tall and sturdy woman seemed to let her guard down, and Sparrow could see the fear in her eyes. "I... can't imagine what she'll do to this nation, to us all. Whatever it is you and Legs are planning, I think you need to do it soon. I'm behind you fully, and I'll see if I can't get some others on our side. Now that we know what's happening... they'll have to listen."

"Let us hope so," Ahmaia said earnestly.

"I'll fly to Legs, let her know," Sparrow said. "Open that window for me?" She veered into her avatar and hopped up onto the sill as Ursa parted the curtains just a little and opened the window. Sparrow was out like a shot. She wasn't the fastest bird, but this news was dire. She'd not stop until she reached Cliffside, not for rest or food.

Sparrow agreed with Ursa. They must act soon, or it would be too late...

...for their House, for the nation, for everyone.

CHAPTER 13

I SAT HEAVILY ON ONE SIDE OF THE LONG COUCH. "THE MISTS? All this for the Mists?" I understood the importance of the Mists and how closely linked Elistan culture was with them, but still. "We invaded a nation, started a war, to claim where the Mists *will be*... in a hundred years?" Something occurred to me then, something Lynx had said about how they'd been sent to claim lands in fear that Vauphan was planning on invading to claim the Mists. The reasoning was very close to the truth, just... that it wasn't Vauphan that planned on moving, but the Mists themselves.

Now it all makes sense, Auwei said. *And I can't believe I didn't know. Shouldn't I have known the Mists were moving?* She sighed. *I guess when I'm within them, I don't really know or care where we are in your realm and when I'm Bonded, I'm usually not close enough to them to tell if they are exactly where they were dozens of years ago. Though...*

What?

Now that I think of it, when showing some of my previous True-Bonded to the Mists, I think that the part of the forest where we entered the Mists was different for some of my earliest hosts than it is now. They are ever-so-slightly further away than they used to be. Fascinating. I've sort of known this entire time, but not really thought anything of it.

Well, someone did think of it and it's causing madness!

Sparrow continued: "Also, Ursa has been tasked with killing all of us and eliminating 'House Maverick.'" She quirked a smile. "Too bad that house doesn't exist anymore."

"How did she seem?" I asked. "Ursa, that is. Is she with us?"

Sparrow shrugged. "She had plenty of opportunity to give me up but didn't. It's possible she's playing a much longer game, but Ahmaia seems to trust her."

I nodded.

I think we can trust her, Auwei chimed in.

Yeah, me too. Thank the Spirits!

"And Merlin is insane," Sparrow added as an afterthought. "I think... she's been behind this all along. I can't be certain, but given how the others deferred to her and the way she was talking, how she acted like she was already the queen—" Sparrow shuddered. "I think if the queen hadn't died, Merlin would have found a way to kill her."

"Great, so we just gave her more power while giving the nation more reason to hate and fear us," I said bitterly. The trouble was, even now, knowing the why behind everything that had been happening, I had no clue what to do. But looking up at Sparrow, small and hopeful, those forest-green eyes seeking some form of acceptance and valida-tion, I smiled. "I'm sorry." I rose and hugged her close. "Thank you. You risked so much, and I can see you're tired. Get some rest. I... I just need to take this all in and think on it."

Her arms went around me, and she held me close. Her

voice was a tremulous whisper when she said, "I was so scared, even though we were hidden. I'm glad I could help."

"You have, so much, thank you."

We held each other close for a long time before drawing back to kiss softly. Then she smiled and retreated to get some rest.

I felt restless. It was already quite dark in the caves, but outside it was early evening, and light enough for a walk. So, I made my way down to the lowest level of the stairs to the rope room. The hooded lantern in the room was lit providing a little light, and the rope ladder was already down, someone was on the beach. Two bright-white scarfs hung on the wall, indicating two people were out. I grabbed another and hung it on a hook. This way if they returned before I did, they wouldn't pull up the ladder. Then I climbed down and walked out of the cave.

I saw the two on the beach, they weren't far away, both sitting on a large rock, looking out over the ocean: Alvere and Silence. Silence had his arm around the other man, as if comforting him.

A part of me wanted to sneak up on them, hear what they were talking about, but I wouldn't betray their trust.

"Hey guys!" I called as I got closer.

They both started and turned their heads back to me. Silence's brown eyes were hard to read, but Alvere's ever-so-clear blue eyes were a bit shocked and... was that ashamed? What had they been talking about? I was curious but wouldn't ask. They'd come to me if they needed me.

They love you, don't worry what they might speak of. Auwei's voice was soft, comforting.

I know, I know.

"I was just going to take a walk down the beach, either or both of you want to join me?"

Alvere smiled, his demeanor changing instantly to bright and cheerful. "I'd love to!" He turned to Silence.

The other man nodded. "As would I."

They rose and came to either side of me, and we clasped hands as we walked.

Silence asked. "Have you heard from Sparrow yet?"

"Yes, she just got back. She's resting. It's because of her news I needed to walk and think." So as to not leave the men in suspense, I told them what Sparrow had told me. Part of me hoped the retelling would spark some ideas for me, but alas, it didn't.

"Vauphan would never think to claim the Mists," Alvere said, bewildered.

"Well, *you* wouldn't, but who knows what some king a hundred years from now might do. I don't approve of any of this, but I can see the twisted logic they used to get to where they are."

Alvere shrugged. "I suppose that's true." He sighed. "All this for... magic, is that it?"

"It's a significant commodity," I said. "Isn't magic the reason your people reached out to the Fey?"

He nodded. "Yes, you're right."

"We have our Mists, you have the Fey, Thraan has dragons, and who knows what other mysterious and wonderful things are out there in the world. Certainly, Thraan has used their dragons to good effect, expanding their empire and dominating the West."

The two men walked in silence. They couldn't dispute what I'd said.

"The Mists are a part of our identity as a nation," I said. "If we didn't have them, we... well we wouldn't be the *same* Elistans we are now."

You wouldn't have me, Auwei whispered.

And that would be a great loss. Have I told you how much I appreciate you?

No, but I can feel it.

Well, I'm telling you anyway, I appreciate The Pits out of you. Without you I'd be...

Normal?

... so very much less than I am now. And not able to help Elista as only I can.

True.

Alvere sighed. "You're right. And given our work with the Fey, they will probably become a part of Vauphan's identity in another few decades." He shook his head. "We're all so driven by power... Why can't we just live in peace?"

"That would be nice," Silence said with a sigh.

"We can live in peace, when we have leaders who make that a priority, and we don't fear our neighbors." I sighed. "There are rumors from the West that Thraan will invade Basia, and if they do, Elista would be next. Which means we always have that in the back of our mind. We need to be prepared for war. I just never thought our war would be with Vauphan." None of this was helping me form a plan of action. "Enough talk of what is," I said. "What can I do? What can *we* do about this?"

More silence.

We watched the shadow of the cliffs to our left spread farther and farther out into the waters. The tide was going out, which was good, since at high tide the waters of the bay would be crashing against those cliffs and we'd not want to be stuck out here. We had at least another hour or so until low tide, which gave us two or three hours until we'd need to be off the beach. I didn't know if it was the news from the capital or the deepening shadows of evening or something else, but I felt my mood slip into darkness. I think Silence and Alvere felt the same.

What could we do?

Obviously, we had to stop Merlin, but she had the entire nation on her side. We had ourselves, few of us that there were, and one other — small — Noble House. And the real trouble was, if we exposed what Merlin was doing, made it public, I honestly wasn't sure how people would feel. They might just support her decisions.

"Even if we tell people what Merlin is doing," Silence said, sounding disheartened, "the nation still might rally around her, not us." He seemed to have read my thoughts.

"I think," Alvere said, pensive, "if you're going to do this right, you need to make less of a deal about the Mists and more about the war. Tell your people Vauphan — the current Vauphan at least — doesn't want war and would be happy to share the Mists. And if we can make peace now, perhaps we can make it last. It isn't that Merlin's *intentions* were wrong, but that her *actions* have cost so many their lives. People need to know that she's killing Elistans and forcing a war which isn't necessary." He gave a breathy laugh. "We thought the why would be important and change everything, but it doesn't. The war and all the deaths are the problem and no matter the reason, they need to stop. Isn't that right?"

Alvere's words had snagged on something in my brain. I was forming an idea, but it was still fuzzy.

"We need to stop the war," I said, trying to form my thoughts into words.

"We need peace," Silence said and that's when it hit me.

Peace.

We needed peace and there was an easy way to do that.

"I know what you need to do," I said, even as my mind was working through this new idea.

"You mean what *we* need to do?" Alvere asked.

"No, what *you* need to do, as The King of Vauphan." And even as I said the next words, as my idea formed, I saw just how truly horrible this solution might be. "You need to show your people and mine that you want peace, that you will do anything for peace, that our countries can come together as allies and share the Mists. You—"

"Legs, no, don't say what I think you're going to say."

But I had to, even if I didn't like it. "You're a king without a queen and we have a queen without a king. Now for us, that's never been an issue, but if you—"

"I'm not marrying that mad woman!" Alvere was adamant. "And I don't know how you could even suggest it!"

"I don't like it either, but don't you see?" I insisted.

"See what? How easily you can throw me away?" Alvere released my hand and turned to me, furious. I couldn't blame him.

"Alvere, no, I love you, but—"

"You love me... but? But what? But you need me to marry an insane megalomaniac to bring peace to our countries?"

"Well maybe you won't have to. Maybe just the proposing of the idea will show Elista that we have nothing to fear from Vauphan."

"Why can't I marry you?" The words flew out of his mouth, and he blinked, surprised.

So was I.

"Is that what you want?" I desperately wanted to know. Because if it was, that would change everything about our relationship. I loved our free and open love, but marriage...

how would that work? Would we have a bunch of mutual lovers we shared in our marriage bed?

"I... I..." he stammered and looked at me and Silence. Then the bluster blew out of him and he shrank down on himself. "I do want that, more than anything. I want to marry you and not have to marry any other. I want to be with you always, even if that means sharing you. But once I'm married, that's it. I can't be with anyone else after that... and neither can the woman I marry."

He turned away. "It's what Silence and I were talking about before you came out." He walked down toward the waterline. "I... I can't stay here forever. This feels like home to me, but I have a country which needs a king. And that king will need a queen and an heir and... By all the gods, I want you to be my queen, but if you were... I don't know if you'd be able to keep these others, whom I know you love as much as you love me. I don't want you to have to give them up, but you would have to change if you were my queen. Otherwise, the line of succession would always be in question."

Damned line of succession. I was so very glad Elista had done away with that many, many years ago.

"I love you, Legs, but..." He gave a self-deprecating, harsh laugh. "Now I'm the one saying 'but.'"

And I saw all of this from his perspective for just a moment: his love for me, but his duty to his country. I couldn't be his queen, no matter how much either of us wanted it. I could be his mistress, his lover, perhaps, but nothing more than that.

What was more, "If you married me, especially now, that would only solidify me and my House as traitors," I said softly, seeing how horrid this truly was. "That wouldn't bring our countries together at all, but divide them all the more."

Yet my plan was sound. "Alvere, I love you and I don't want to lose you, but don't you see? You have it in your power to start the peace process. Even just suggesting the idea will show your people and mine how much you want peace, which means if Merlin turns you down, it will show them how much she wants war."

"And what if she accepts?" Alvere said sourly.

Spirits, I couldn't imagine what he'd go through if he actually married that woman.

He went on, tone still bitter. "Legs, I can see where you're going, but there is one flaw. If Merlin accepts my proposal, she could very easily turn that to her benefit. She becomes the benevolent peacemaker. She could blame the war on you or the previous queen and say this is what she wants. That wouldn't achieve what we want at all. There would be peace, but the maniacs in power would still be in power. And..." He shuddered. "Once I'd given her an heir, I wouldn't be needed. She could easily do away with me and control both countries. I'd be dead and nothing would have changed except we'd have handed Vauphan to Merlin!"

I nodded. "You're right."

"But..." Silence drew out the word. Alvere and I both turned to him. "What if it became known that Maverick House didn't betray Elista? What if everyone was told that we were the ones who began the peace talks?"

He didn't seem entirely sure of his idea, but continued. "I don't know how we'd spread the rumors, but... we could suggest that our House went to make peace with the Vauphani and were betrayed by our own... who didn't want peace?" He was still questioning his own idea.

Then suddenly Silence blinked and lit up. "Yes! Something like… Vauphan is suing for peace, at the behest of Maverik House, now Spider House, and the prince wants to come in person to seal the alliance. A Royal marriage isn't out of the question, *but* only after the question of how the war started is put to all the Nobles of Elista… because… someone in Elista tried to sabotage our house from pursuing peace. We act like we don't know who that was, and we just want to come before all the Nobles to work out what's going on. That way, Alvere could bring us into the peace talks with him, not as traitors, but as peacemakers. And yes, Merlin could spread rumors about us being traitors, but that would make her seem like the warmonger. Wouldn't that work?"

I thought about it. There was something in that idea. It was close, it had something to do with putting Merlin in a corner. If she wanted peace, she'd have to acknowledge us as peacemakers, not traitors, and if she didn't want peace, she'd be seen as the warmonger. Yet…

"There is still a lot that could go wrong with that," I said slowly. "It all depends on who is on her side and loyal to her. She could have one of her allies, Fang or whoever is the new leader of Panther House, call for war and claim we're traitors, that way she stays clean and untouchable." I sighed. "And there really isn't anything stopping the other Nobles from thinking we *were* traitors, who saw that we'd lose the war so we changed our tactics to peace. That *is*, sort of what we're doing. How do we prove we've always wanted the best for Elista?"

"What about Ursa?" Silence said.

"Ursa," I said, repeating the name. I sighed heavily. We'd trusted her so far. Could we continue to do so? I'd rather not put all our eggs into that one basket, but…

A smile spread slowly on my face. "Yes, Ursa."

Auwei giggled. *I sense a crazy plan coming on!*

"You have an idea?" Alvere said. I could hear the hope in his voice, he didn't want our time together to end, even though we both knew it would have to, someday.

"Yes..." I spoke slowly as the plan clarified in my mind. "You send a letter to Merlin and tell her you want peace, that a political alliance, perhaps a marriage of some sort is on the table, *but* you won't make any decisions until the new queen or king of Elista is elected."

"Right!" Alvere breathed.

"Oh, yes!" Silence said at the same time.

It seemed we'd all forgotten that Merlin wasn't officially queen yet. She had to be elected first.

"Tell Merlin you would like to come to peace talks, but only if all the Nobles are gathered and have a say on the outcome, that you want to see the election process."

"But wait, what if the Nobles actually do elect Merlin?" Alvere asked.

"That's where Ursa comes in. *Before* those talks, a small group of us go with Ursa to several Nobles whom she thinks we can trust. You go with her, tell your story. I don't know yet if it would be wise to have me there or not, but we can figure that out. If we can sway four Noble Houses, then that would create a stalemate at least. That's assuming the Nobles *don't* let me vote, which I'd expect."

But in the case of a stalemate the current Royal House is the tie-breaker, Auwei added in.

So my plan's not perfect, but it's close. Perhaps we can flip more than four houses? Who knows. Or perhaps they'll let me vote.

That's unlikely.

Still... do you have a better plan?

... No.

Well then?

I'm just trying to temper your expectations.

Consider them tempered.

"I think the best outcome we can expect is that with so many Houses voting against her, Merlin gets angry and exposes her true nature," I said. "That might sway things further in our favor."

If she is truly mad that may not be too hard. That might actually work.

Thank you.

I turned to Alvere, taking the few steps to close the distance between us. "Well, what do you think?"

He sighed. "I think I still love you and I'm still going to have to marry another and that breaks my heart."

It broke mine too.

But that was a battle for another day.

I embraced him and felt his strong arms around me. "We'll figure something out," I said.

Alvere said nothing, just held me all the tighter.

CHAPTER 14

My plan had a lot of moving parts, and we used Fin a lot.

First Alvere went home to the capital of Vauphan and drafted his letter to Merlin, but he was delayed there as several matters of state had to be addressed. In the meantime, Ursa and I went to see Lord War in his makeshift prison behind the Vauphani battle lines up north.

"I won't tell you anything, you filthy bitch!" War spat at me, before turning back into a wasp and buzzing angrily around his enclosure, pushing against the fine mesh netting which had been put in place around the dual cage.

Eorthan, the metal wielding Fey had outdone himself on this structure, an internal cage with fine, yet strong bars in a lattice which had square holes no larger than a couple inches across. No part of Lord War could reach through gaps that small except his fingers. Then there was a second, outer cage — perhaps six inches out from the first — of the same material and lattice, and around that was the mesh netting. If War changed into his avatar and slipped through the inner cage he'd be stopped by the netting, but he didn't have enough room to return to himself between the two cages, so he'd not be able to rip a hole in the netting to escape through.

"You don't have to say anything to me," I said with a grin, "But the Nobles will want to hear your side of the story when we choose a new monarch. So, we're taking you with us. As a peace offering."

He transformed back and smiled, a devilish thing. "Oh?" I could see the gears turning in his head. If we let him out, he could escape, and even if he didn't, we were taking him back to his mad master, she'd free him.

I moved away from the cage with Ursa.

"He radiates deceit," she whispered. "Even without my abilities, I'd probably be able to tell when he was lying. I can see how you intend to use him, but how will you keep him in line and restrained for that long?"

I grinned. "Follow me."

We went to another section of the camp, to Eorthan's forge. I recalled when Alvere gave me my unique Fey armor, which I was currently wearing. I ran my hands over the moving metal and smiled.

"How's it going?" I asked Eorthan.

The small man shrugged. "I don't have willing subjects to test them on, so I'm glad you're here. There are three sets over there, I'm hoping one of them works." He pointed to the side table. Ursa and I looked to see three sets of manacles.

"I'll try them on!" I said excited.

Ursa looked at me. "You want to be chained up?"

I laughed. "I want to make sure these will work. Eorthan has been using Fey magic to see if he can make manacles that can stop a True-Bonded from veering into their avatar."

"That's horrible!" Ursa gasped.

I have to agree, Auwei said, disturbed. *They may also cut off our connection.*

I guess we'll see. Sorry if they do, but this is necessary.

I know, but I don't have to like it.

To Ursa I said, "These will be necessary if we want to get Lord War from here to wherever without him escaping."

She nodded reluctantly to that.

Ursa and Eorthan helped me into the first set.

Are you there Auwei?

Yes.

So... not cut off. Then I wonder if I can veer?

I veered into my spider form and the manacles fell away, thumping to the ground. That was an interesting start. Usually everything I had on me would shift with me, which might have included the manacles but they'd remained autonomous. Still, they hadn't stopped me.

With the second set, I felt an indescribable resistance to shifting, but it was still possible. I told Eorthan as much. Also speaking to Auwei was possible, but our communication was sort of slurred and difficult, as if we were two drunken people trying to shout at each other.

He nodded. "I used different aspects of the nature of steel to imbue them, this one focused on steel's resilience. The last set might work. I focused my crafting into the steel's generally unchangeable nature."

"But steel is changeable," Ursa said. "You made it into manacles, isn't that changeable?"

"Only at high temperatures. So, you'd have to heat the manacles to a very uncomfortable heat to overcome their magic."

"Ah." She nodded.

I tried on the last set.

Auwei?

No response. Curious.

When I tried to veer, nothing happened. "It worked!" I said, excited. "Here, Ursa, try them on, I want to make sure they'll work on anyone."

Once I removed them Auwei gasped. *That was horrible, like being in a cold dark place. I couldn't sense anything from you at all!*

Was it different from when Hale cut off our connection?

Yes, very. Then I was still a part of you, I just couldn't reach you. This was like being torn away from you entirely.

I'm sorry you had to go through that.

I know it was necessary, but let's not do that again, shall we?

Agreed.

Ursa was hesitant, but saw the need to test the manacles and did as asked. She too, couldn't change with them on. She tried to use her extreme strength to break the manacles, but only succeeded in wearing herself out and hurting her wrists.

"They work," she admitted, then grunted a sour, "Ow."

That was another part of my plan in place. The next bit would be the hardest yet.

Fin returned Ursa and me to Cliffside and then was off to wait for Alvere to be done to return him here as well. I met with Dove and Ursa in my room.

The plan was for Fin to take Alvere, Ursa, and Dove to some of the Nobles we thought we could trust. Already Grizzly himself had talked to Tanuki, and she seemed on board with the plan, but we'd stop in to see her, just to verify. We also would speak with Spike, the leader of Porcupine house. Fin could get us close to that one, since it was further up the eastern coast of Elista. After that... we'd try with Wyvern and possibly Pegasus. Those were the two risky ones.

"I'll be there, every step of the way with you," I said to my sister. I would go along too, but in avatar form, hidden among their clothes. As long as Hale didn't make an appearance, I'd be fine.

"Are you sure we should be visiting Lady Silvermane?" Dove asked, worried. "We know Lord Horn sides with his son and it would be nearly impossible to get a meeting with Silvermane without Horn there." Even though these were members of the House she'd once been a part of, I could see the fear in her eyes. She was a strong woman, but the betrayal she'd endured when Hale had accosted her... had left deep scars. It was hard for her to trust anyone outside of myself and my House.

"I could do that one with just King Alvere," Ursa said.

"No, I think Silvermane needs to hear Dove's story. From what Sparrow told us, Silvermane never believed Dove to be a traitor. Hale convinced her I'd stolen my sister away. She's always hoped to free Dove and bring her back home."

Dove nodded. "I'll go." I could see her strength, her bravery in the face of her fear, putting herself potentially in harm's way.

I nodded. "Once Fin is back, we'll visit Tanuki first and confirm her allegiance. Then to Porcupine House and Spike. I don't think he'll be in Merlin's sway, so hopefully he'll be easier to bring to our side. After that to the capital and Skyfire and Silvermane." I sighed. "I just don't know which one to do first. If the first goes badly, we'll have to flee and won't be able to do the second."

We all considered for a moment. I spoke my thoughts aloud: "Both Skyfire and Silvermane were with the queen the day of her speech. That doesn't mean anything per-se, but..." I shrugged.

"Silvermane might be willing to listen to Dove, but she

may also think you killed her mother," Ursa advised. "That might not go well."

"So Silvermane could be good or bad, depending on which way she leans. She might believe Dove but still not trust me." I sighed. "That doesn't help us. Skyfire is a complete enigma. So, I guess the question is, do we do the complete mystery first, or the one where we have some intel, but it could go either way?"

"Do Silvermane first," Dove said resolutely. "I'll convince her."

"Are you sure?" I asked.

Dove nodded.

That was it. We were set.

CHAPTER 15

OUR MEETINGS WITH TANUKI AND SPIKE WENT WELL. THEY were on board, on our side. I allowed myself to feel just a little confident that everything would work out. Three Houses had sided with us. That alone was a significant triumph. But now came the hard ones: Pegasus and Wyvern. We needed one of the two with us if we wanted to be sure of a stalemate, both if we wanted a victory. These meetings would make or break my plans.

As such, we wanted to be ready and rested before we went in, staying for a day — hidden away in a small inn — in the capital before we went to see Silvermane.

I spent the day with Alvere. I wouldn't see him much after this, so we sat together and talked the hours away. Dove and Fin did much the same in the next room. I'd happily noted how they'd been spending more time together. I was glad my sister had found someone. Fin was a big man, but gentle and caring. I wished them well.

Ursa, being the only one of us who could move freely around the capital, went out to gather what information she could. She didn't discover anything of note.

The next day, we went to see Silvermane.

I was hidden underneath Alvere's cloak as our group was escorted into Silvermane's sitting room. The cloak hampered my spider's ability to sense things around me, but I knew Lord Horn was in the room when he spoke first.

"Lady Ursa, we were expecting only you, not such a group as this and cloaked against the world. Who are these others?" His tone was accusing.

I heard a gasp, then Silvermane's soft voice. "Dove!"

"Yes, Lady, and this is the King of Vauphan. He comes to talk of peace."

"Hello, my Lady." I heard Alvere's voice, felt the rumble of it in his chest, and the motion of his arms as he removed his hood.

"This last is a guard for the King," Ursa said, indicating Fin. That was his cover. The large man was wearing heavy armor including a helm to hide his identity. He hated the armor, saying it chafed something fierce, but he'd agreed to it.

"The King of Vauphan?" Lady Silvermane's voice sounded shocked. "This I had not expected when you'd asked for a private meeting, Lady Ursa."

I crawled up Alvere's back, high enough so I could be free of his cloak. I felt his shiver — I'm sure having a spider walk up his back had been... interesting — but he settled quickly. I didn't need to peer over his shoulder, just be free of the cloak, then my senses were free to take in the room. The four from my delegation were still just inside the door. Lady Silvermane sat behind a large desk with Horn standing behind her. A large bank of windows occupied the wall behind them.

Silvermane rose and came around the desk to embrace

Dove. "I was so worried about you. Your sister... what we've heard..."

Dove embraced her former leader. "Thank you for your concern, Lady. However, what you have heard is mostly rumor and lies, but we'll get to that shortly. The King should speak first."

"Yes, of course," Silvermane said, and I sensed her going to Alvere. She curtseyed, offering her hand, which he took and bowed his head, though his lips didn't quite touch her knuckles. "Your Majesty."

"Lady, thank you for seeing us. I apologize for the subterfuge in Lady Ursa's message, but it was necessary. Unfortunately, we do not know who we can trust here in Elista. As Lady Dove has said, there are far too many rumors and lies about. I am here to hopefully clear up some of those and to tell you of my proposal for peace." With his hand still holding hers, she guided him to a chair and he sat. Silvermane returned to her chair behind the desk. Dove sat next to the King, and Ursa stood behind her. Fin stood behind the king, a looming presence. I felt a perilous tension from everyone in the room, but most of all Lord Horn. He would be the wildcard in this meeting.

"Say your piece," Silvermane said, voice just a little cool. That wasn't a good start, but at least she was willing to listen.

"What do you know of the war in the North?" Alvere began.

I heard Silvermane's heavy breath. "I have heard many things," she said, enigmatically. "Mostly I heard how a force from Vauphan somehow crossed into our camp and slew or captured all of the high Nobles of House Panther. I've also heard of mysterious magics which hinder our men from wearing or wielding steel. Do you deny this?"

"No, I do not," Alvere said evenly. "But I ask, did you hear of the attack on the Vauphani camp which prompted our counterattack?"

"No," she said, hesitant and curious.

"As I suspected." Alvere's tone was even, not accusing. "Lady, please understand I do not wish for this war, I—"

"Then why did you start it?" Horn said, hard and cold.

I felt Alvere's calming breath. "Lord Horn, I hope you will listen to my full story. If you do, you will see, not only did I not wish for this war, but Vauphan did not start it either."

"That's a lie," Horn said, voice growing heated.

"Horn, let him speak." This from Silvermane, who didn't sound convinced, but again seemed willing to listen.

"Thank you, Lady. From what we have gathered, most of those in Elista have heard the following about the war: That Vauphan was either planning an invasion or had already attacked. Your Panther House responded to these actions or expected actions by pre-emptively seizing Vauphan lands, or defending themselves then claiming those lands to stop any further attacks. Does that sound right to you?"

"It does," Silvermane said.

"And when did this start?"

"About a year ago, if I recall correctly," Silvermane replied.

"What if I told you the war began almost *three* years ago?" Alvere said cautiously.

"That seems a bit preposterous." Lady Silvermane laughed. "I would have heard something in such a case."

"Indeed. Then let me begin my tale a bit more recently. Were you aware that a mistweaver, sent by your government, attacked and killed my mother and father?"

"Legs is a mistweaver?" Silvermane gasped. "Your sister... I..."

"Lady, no, that is not the case," Dove said firmly. "You believe my sister killed the king and queen of Vauphan?"

"Why yes," she said, as if it were the obvious truth. "She was sent to spy and went rogue, killing the royals."

"And in this matter, would you admit that I may know more than you, as to the events?" Alvere asked. "I was there that night. I saw it with my own eyes." That was a bit of an exaggeration, but close enough to the truth.

"Yes, of course," Silvermane acquiesced. "You say it was a mistweaver? And... not Legs-the-traitor?"

"That is indeed the case," Alvere said evenly.

"I find that hard to believe," Horn said with a scoff. "A mistweaver? You speak of fairy tales."

"My Lord, respectfully, a mistweaver did indeed attack my parents, and she was not sent by Maverick House, as you may believe. No, in fact, it was Lady Legs who stopped the mistweaver, saving my life."

A silence hung in the room.

"I find that even harder to believe," Horn said after a moment. "Mistweavers are legends for a reason. They were nigh unstoppable. And you want us to believe a novice Noble stopped this mistweaver?"

It *was* hard to believe. Even I had trouble believing it some days, and I'd been the one to do it!

"Legs had help." Another small lie. "Others from her House were there and together they defeated the mist-weaver. As you say, they were at the palace to spy, of that I am aware. I was not impressed by that, but I was willing to forgive, given they saved my life from that same mistweaver. If we can start with this as fact, does that change anything of what you might believe?"

"What you say is hard to believe, Your Majesty." Silver-mane sighed. "But for now, we shall take your word on this. Assuming this to be true, what followed?"

Alvere's shoulder's fell in a heavy sigh. He'd cleared the first hurdle, if only just. "Follow my logic for a moment if you will," he said. Then he launched into an impassioned argument. "If indeed it wasn't House Maverick who sent the mistweaver, but who stopped it, then..." He let that hang for a moment. "Then, who sent the mistweaver?"

"Perhaps they were acting alone?" Horn's voice was hard. He still didn't believe any of this. "Your nation began a war and perhaps they sought to end it in one go."

A sudden shift in Alvere told me he felt his tenuous hold on the two before him slipping away. "This is silly," Ursa said finally. "Lady Silvermane, are you aware of my spirit-gift?"

Oh, thank the Spirits.

"Your spirit-gift? No."

"I have the ability to discern truth from lies. To prove it, I ask you to tell me five things. Make some truths and some lies, and I shall tell you which is which."

I sensed Silvermane's hesitation. A stifling silence hung heavy in the room, but finally Silvermane broke it. "As you wish." She drew in a long breath. "First, Lord Horn and I are lovers. Second, I have a daughter, which I have hidden from the world. Third, I am currently pregnant. Fourth I hate my mother for pushing me so hard as a child. And finally, I want to kill Legs for killing my mother. How's that?" The hotness of her voice was evident, along with a tremulous nervousness. I got the sense she never would have said half these things otherwise.

"Oh..." Ursa sounded stunned and apologetic. "My Lady, I am sorry for making you go through this. That couldn't have been easy for you. The first three things you said are all true, the last two are lies.

Wait... Lord Horn — a man who was well more than twice her age — was Silvermane's lover? No wonder she'd never taken a husband. And Horn had gotten her with child twice? Fascinating. But that also meant she didn't hate her mother and didn't want to kill me. Odd, I would have thought killing me would have been a priority if she thought I killed her mother.

Silvermane sighed heavily. "Indeed, that is correct." She cleared her throat quickly. "And I do not wish to discuss any of that, and I hope you will all keep it in the strictest confidence."

"Of course, Lady," Alvere said quickly.

That oppressive silence dominated the room once again, before Ursa remembered to speak. "I trust I have proven myself?"

"Yes. Go on."

"Do you trust me to evaluate the truth of what the King is saying?"

"How do we know you're not in league with him?" Horn said skeptically. There was no convincing him. Though perhaps he was angry at what the woman he loved had just been put through.

Ursa sighed heavily. "Do you want this war?" she asked directly. "Our people are dying. Some of your Nobles are at the front now. Do you want them to die if this continues?" Before he could answer she pushed on. "Then you'll need to trust someone at some point, and if you can't trust me, another second from another Noble House, then whom can you trust?"

The trouble was, I knew who he trusted. He trusted his

son and his lover and that was probably it. Still, I waited for his reply and hoped.

Horn let out a grunt then said, "Perhaps I will trust you, but first, tell me this. How did you come to know the King? How did Dove come to be in your care? All of this rings a little too much of the work of someone else."

"I presume you mean the work of the traitor Noble House once known as Maverick?" Ursa said easily. I didn't like that phrasing, but I was in no position to argue.

"Yes."

Ursa sighed. "You want the full and honest truth, then fine. Know that we are not here to hurt you, only to talk, so please don't be alarmed. Legs, please come out."

I hoped she knew what she was doing. I hopped off Alvere's shoulder and returned to myself in mid-jump, landing lightly and bowing to Lady Silvermane and Lord Horn.

"Your Ladyship, Your Lordship."

The room froze in a tense tableau. Silvermane and Horn wore expressions which were both surprised and not surprised at the same time. As if my appearance confirmed their suspicions about this meeting, but they were still shocked that I'd dared to show my face.

"Trust us or not," Ursa said softly, but sternly. "We only ask that you listen, then let us go. Will you abide by those terms?"

Silvermane nodded, looking a bit dumbfounded.

"Your Ladyship, no!" Horn hissed. "We can't let her go! She must pay for what she did to your mother!"

"I did not kill the queen," I said quickly.

"The truth," Ursa confirmed.

"How can we trust you? Any of you?" Horn bit out.

"Again, Lord Horn, you don't have to, just listen. Then we'll be gone." Ursa's tone was hard. "Do you agree."

"Yes," Silvermane whispered. "I have to know..." Her voice barely a breath. "If you didn't kill my mother, who did?"

"A mistweaver," Dove said for me. "A curse had been placed on the queen. She died as soon as she left the capital."

"And yes, taking her from the capital was my doing," I said. "But I had no clue that would kill her. I just needed to speak to her. I am so very sorry."

"All truths," Ursa said.

"A mistweaver? They're real?" Silvermane looked terrified.

"Yes." The word came from myself, Alvere, and Dove at once.

Silvermane blinked for a moment. She looked like she didn't believe any of this, but she nodded. "Go on, say your piece, then leave." Her tone, though quiet, was hard. She didn't like any of this, that was obvious.

I took up the telling from there. "The mistweaver sent to kill the Vauphani king and queen, had also been tasked with killing me. It seemed I would get in the way of someone's plans. At the time I didn't know what those plans were, I was only trying to survive. I did indeed kill the mistweaver, though I nearly died myself. That is how I came to know the prince, now King of Vauphan. We have only ever wanted peace between our two nations, but someone else is behind this war." I couldn't go into specifics, not yet.

I hoped Silvermane would see it for herself when the time came for the Council of Nobles. So, I left things vague. "Someone on our side, someone in Elista, started this war. They know the Mists are moving and will eventually migrate into Vauphan, and they wished to take the lands in the North of Vauphan to protect our Mists, a noble but misguided goal. Vauphan would never have cut us off from our heritage. The King is here to say exactly that and to offer a political alliance. He will come to the Council of Nobles, and whoever is chosen as the new king or queen will be bound to him, either to marry or for their children to marry, thus bringing our nations together and ending all this needless bloodshed. I have never betrayed Elista, but someone high up in the Royal house must be involved in this plot and has been spreading foul rumors about me. I stole my sister away from the capital as I feared she might be in danger." That was true, I just wouldn't mention Lord Hale specifically.

"Yes, we fought against our own kind, fighting for Vauphan at the front lines, but I'm willing to bet you didn't know Lord War was there, and it was him and Jaguar who attacked us first, killing Maverick and several Nobles of his House. Our attack on their camp was only to stop the fighting, end the hostilities, which were initiated by the Elistan side. Believe me or not, but you'll see the truth of things at the Council of Nobles." I paused, a bit out of breath. I looked at Alvere and Dove. "Did I miss anything?"

"How did Ursa get involved?" Horn asked.

I nodded. "I had a friend from Silverveil who is now a member of Grizzly House. I went to her to ask for help. She brought me to Ursa, who used her abilities to determine I was truthful and agreed to help me."

Silvermane looked a little confused. "So... you killed the mistweaver that cast a curse on my mother?"

"I hope I am being honest when I say: yes. I cannot be certain. I killed *a* mistweaver. There may be another one, but I hope to the Spirits there isn't." I shrugged. "So... it seems likely that I killed the one who cast the curse upon your mother."

Silvermane nodded.

"That is a fanciful tale," Horn said, clearly not believing it.

"We shall consider what you have told us," Silvermane said. "Now, please leave."

That was not how I had hoped this would go, but we weren't being apprehended or chased out, so it definitely could have gone worse.

"Thank you for your time," I said, then we all linked to Fin and were gone from Silvermane's office.

We returned to the room we'd rented in the city.

"Do we go to Skyfire?" Ursa asked. "Horn may be warning others even as we speak."

"Then we go quickly," I said.

Ursa nodded.

CHAPTER 16

IT SEEMED WYVERN HOUSE HAD NOT BEEN WARNED, AT LEAST not yet. We were admitted to Lady Skyfire's study.

Yet even as Fin closed the door behind us and Ursa was about to speak, Lord Drake, Skyfire's second, hissed: "Legs is with them, on the back of the short male. It's a trick, a trap!" How he knew, I had no clue, but it threw everything into chaos.

Hidden under Alvere's cloak, I didn't see what happened next. I felt the cloak being ripped off Alvere as he was pushed to one side...

...By Lady Skyfire herself.

Faster than I could see, she plucked me off the man's back, holding me by one of my tiny legs, careful not to crush it, but precise enough to hold just the one small limb.

"Show yourself!" she commanded.

I couldn't believe *this* was how I'd finally meet my childhood idle.

I shifted back to myself and Skyfire had one of my hands grasped in hers, bound in a grip like iron.

"I have you now, traitor!" she hissed.

"Wait!" Ursa's strong voice stopped everyone. The tall woman stalked over to Skyfire. "This is no trap."

For a long moment the two powerful women squared off. Ursa was taller, but Skyfire had an intensity about her, which made up for the difference. Both were powerfully built and strong. Steel-blue eyes met fiery-orange eyes.

"Who do you serve?" Ursa asked quickly. "Merlin or Elista?"

"Merlin?" Skyfire scoffed. "Never. She's a wimp who's inherited her power. She'll be out after the next Council. I serve Elista. Who do *you* serve?"

"I serve Elista," Ursa said. Then she looked to me and added, "She's telling the truth."

Skyfire looked back and forth between us, flame-red hair bouncing around as she did so. "Of course I'm telling the truth." To Ursa she countered, "What is the meaning of this? Bringing a traitor into my House?"

"I do apologize for the subterfuge, but she couldn't walk in here on her own, now could she? She and The King of Vauphan have something they'd like to say to you."

"The King of... what? Where?" She looked at Fin in his armor. "Are you—?"

"No, my Lady," Drake said cutting her off. "The small one. I can see it now."

Still holding my arm Skyfire turned to Alvere. "You're the King of Vauphan?" I could tell she was off balance now.

"Yes, Lady Skyfire. It's a pleasure to meet you," Alver said, calm and genial.

She glared at him. "What's going on here?" she said, her temper — which was notoriously short — clearly rising. I felt her hand leave my wrist, but at the same time she became a blur, moving around the room so fast I couldn't follow her. Even before my arm had fallen an inch, she had it again. Then both my arms were wrenched behind my back and I was moved — so fast I couldn't see a thing — to the other side of the room. I found myself in Drake's hands as he pulled a dagger, putting it to my throat. Somehow, during that flash of movement, Skyfire had bound my wrists together.

Wow.

"There!" Skyfire said with a huff. "Now I feel better. Someone better explain things quickly or you'll all end up like Legs here." She sat behind her desk and leaned back in her chair, clearly in control.

Even in my very precarious position I admired her power and authority. She dominated this room, even though she was outnumbered. She smiled with easy confidence as she stared down Ursa — a powerful Noble, in both position and physique — and the King of Vauphan. A part of me — the part not freaking out about being captured and having a knife at my throat, nor the part that was still a little sick from being moved so quickly — was giddy at being so close to this amazing woman!

You really admire her, don't you? Auwei asked.

I have all my life. If there was one person I wanted to be... it was her.

I'm sorry you didn't meet under better circumstances.

Yeah... me to.

Ursa recovered quickly. "May I sit?" she asked, motioning to a chair.

"Whatever," Skyfire said with a wave of her hand. "Just get talking!"

Ursa took a chair. Alvere sat in another. Dove and Fin

stayed close behind the other two. I could see the concern in Dove's eyes, but some part of me hoped this would all work out, and I gave her a reassuring wink. I wasn't worried... yet. Ursa had said Skyfire was telling the truth about not serving Merlin, which meant we had a chance.

"I know we don't know each other well," Ursa began. "But I'd like to think we know each other well enough to trust each other?"

"I did, until you brought a traitor into my study," Skyfire countered.

"And who said she was a traitor? Merlin?"

"Yes, as well as half the nation. Why do you keep mentioning Merlin?"

"I'll get to that. First, why I'm here. To introduce you to the King of Vauphan. He wishes to discuss terms of peace. He is hoping to be at the Council of Nobles to propose that Vauphan and Elista be joined in marriage, either through him or his children. That way there is no need for war. What do you think of this?"

"Sure, peace is good. As long as I don't have to marry him." Skyfire surveyed the king. "He's a little scrawny, not my type."

"Do you wish to be the next queen?" Ursa asked.

"Not really your business, but no. I'll take it, if I'm the only choice, but I'd rather not. I like my life as it is."

"Would you support Merlin as queen?"

"Pits no!" Skyfire seemed disgusted by the idea. "I'd like to think we have other options than her. She hasn't done much to impress me." All of this was sounding positive. Skyfire definitely wasn't on Merlin's side. Now we just had to convince her to join our side. "Why all the talk of who's going to be queen?"

"That would be very important to me," Alvere said.

Skyfire grunted. "Yeah, I suppose it would. So, if a queen is chosen for Elista you'll marry her, and if not, your kids and the chosen king's kids will hook up?"

"That is the plan, yes." Alvere remained calm, though I caught his furtive glances in my direction.

"The King's in love with Legs," Drake said behind me.

How in The Pits did he know these things? Did he have a spirit-gift like Ursa's?

"Really? The traitor? I heard she went over to your side. Now I know why."

Alvere sighed. "I do love her, but I'll do what I must for my country." He spoke up a little more. "And while we're on the topic, one of the reasons why I love her is that she saved my life from a mistweaver who killed my father and mother, the king and queen." He then stared directly at Drake when he said: "Is that a lie?"

Skyfire looked at Drake.

I couldn't see the man who was holding me, so I waited, curious what was taking him so long to answer.

"I do not believe you are lying, no. But something about this whole meeting is out of place." He paused for a moment. "You, the woman behind Ursa, you're Lady Dove are you not?"

Spirits this man was keen. He seemed to know everything.

"Truly?" Skyfire turned and looked at Dove. "Is that who you are?"

"Yes," Dove said with a bow. "We just came from telling Silvermane what we're telling you, that Legs isn't a traitor. We believe Merlin to be the one who is destroying our country."

"She is earnest," Drake said.

"Well Bloody Pits!" Skyfire leaned back again. "Who do I believe?"

"Lady," Drake said firmly, and I felt the dagger at my throat pull away a little. "I believe them to be honest. I do not think Legs will harm us, nor any of the rest of them, and... my apologies for not mentioning it sooner, but I fear Lady Merlin is quite insane. I have not seen her enough to know for certain. She hides it well, but I've suspected as much for some time."

"And you didn't tell me because...?"

"I wanted to be sure."

"That our *queen* is off her rocker? I think we could have gone with a hunch on that one." Skyfire threw her arms into the air. "Fine! Let her go."

Drake removed the dagger and used it to cut my bonds.

"Thank you," I said to him with a smile. He nodded to me. It was only then, as his pale brown eyes met mine, that I saw how keenly he looked at me. Was that his gift? He could "see" things? His eyes did seem to take in everything, keen and alert.

Curious.

I made my way around to rejoin my friends as Skyfire said, "So, you think Merlin is the traitor? What has she done?"

We told her everything we knew about the mistweaver and the war and Ursa's meeting with Merlin... and the Mists.

Then we stood back and waited.

"You sure these aren't the crazy ones?" she asked Drake.

"I see no betrayal, even if their words are hard to believe," he said reluctantly.

Ha! So, it *was* something with his sight!

"Well, Pits!" Skyfire said. "Isn't this just fantastic!" She rose and began pacing.

I also paced! We were so alike!

She's a bit erratic, and you're not. You may have some similarities, but you are also very different. I like you a lot better.

You would say that, you're my Lumani. You're stuck with me... also, thanks.

"You've given me a lot to think about," Skyfire said, not looking at us. "I'm assuming I'll see you again at the Council of Nobles?"

"Yes," I said.

"Well, I'm not sure I'm with you, but I'm definitely not with Merlin. Personally, I think you're both crazy. You'll have my answer then," she said.

And that was that.

Before we left, I couldn't help myself, I went to Skyfire. "I just wanted to say, I've always admired you and looked up to you."

"Well yeah, of course you did." Skyfire sniffed.

You also don't have an outrageously large ego, Auwei said.

Yeah... wow.

I turned away, a bit put out by this, but Skyfire called me back. "Hey, kid."

I turned around.

She smiled. "Your House may be tiny, but you're the youngest House leader ever. That ain't nothing." She gave me a wink.

I smiled and nodded at the compliment, my giddiness at meeting her returning.

We left and returned to Cliffside.

That was it. We didn't know how Silvermane or Skyfire would vote, but at least they knew the facts, even if they might not believe them. I had to hope that would be enough.

The Council was called a few days later. It would be in Miraline in two weeks.

Two weeks and everything would come to a head.

I couldn't wait, anxious and fidgety.

Luckily, I had several people willing to distract me.

CHAPTER 17

IT STARTED INNOCENTLY ENOUGH. I WAS A TENSE WRECK —
pacing around the common area — so Ant offered to give
me a massage. I lay on the long couch, and he dug those
thick, strong fingers into my shoulders, neck, and back until
I'd turned to mush with contentment.

It was only once he'd finished and risen from straddling
my legs, that I turned my head to see the heavy bulge in his
breeches.

"It looks like you could use a massage too," I purred.

"I wouldn't turn one down." His voice was husky, deep
and needful.

I rose, but he quickly swept me off my feet, cradling me
high in his arms. I wrapped my hands around his neck to
pull my face to his for a long and probing kiss. Then he
carefully carried me down to my room.

As we reached the lower landing, Silence was coming up
from the beach-exit. Alvere was back home in Vauphan,
ruling his nation and planning for the upcoming summit.
Sparrow was off scouting, as she and Dove often did, to
ensure our secret base remained a secret.

Silence raised a brow. Ant nodded, so Silence followed us to my room.

Apparently, my guys could communicate with only their expressions now.

Once inside, Ant set me down and the two men slowly undressed me. Their hands — one set hard, thick, and strong, the other soft, nimble, and quick — moved over fabric, then under, as my blouse and skirt were removed. Then I went from one to the other, kissing and caressing one while the other quickly stripped. And when they were naked, they sandwiched me between them, skin pressing to skin.

Silence had spent our time in exile improving his combat skills and it had made his muscles fuller and harder, but still nothing compared to Ant. Yet with the two hard bodies pressed against me I was already in heaven.

"What do you need?" Silence asked in a whisper, kissing around my ear from behind.

"Ant needs a release first, then I want to forget about everything for a while." I hadn't forgotten the reason for coming down here. Ant had already given me a wonderful massage and now he needed something in return.

"Allow me," Silence said and gently moved me out of the way, going to his knees in front of Ant, taking that Oh-My-Spirits sized erection in his hand and bringing it to his lips.

Ant's eyes never left me as I moved to the bed and lay down. I opened my legs so he could watch me stroke myself. My other hand traced over my body, coming to a breast, pleasuring myself, feeling the tight bud of a nipple and flicking it playfully.

Ant, it seemed, didn't need much encouragement and was soon having full body contractions, bending him slightly as he found his release. His gaze never left me.

When Silence went to the pitcher of water on the small table in my room for a drink, Ant came to me, kneeling beside the bed and pulling me close to press his lips to my wet folds. Hard hands grabbed my hips to push his face in closer as he sated his hunger and spiked my desire. I ran my hands through the tight black curls on his head, raising my hips to welcome him deeper. My body moved to the rhythm of his lips and tongue, my back arching, eyelids fluttering, and eyes rolled back as Ant's incessant hunger nearly drove me mad.

The bed shifted. I glanced over to see Silence next to me. He lay propped up on an arm, leaning over so his free hand and lips could find my breasts. The delicate and delicious suction of his mouth upon the already aroused bud of my nipple was all I needed to find a body-shivering orgasm, tensing with tremors of delight. I let go and rode the waves of pleasure these two glorious men were inciting.

Silence's lips found mine, playing and pulling, sucking and sliding. I reached out with a hand, fumbling and finding his erection, rigid and ready. I gripped it tight and heard his corresponding grunt of pained pleasure.

At the same time Ant's amazing lips left my folds, and a moment later I felt the probing tip of his erection, aroused once again. The heavy press of his length slid over my more-than-ready opening and though I couldn't see, I assumed he was directing it, playing. It slapped down hard upon my engorged clit a couple of times prompting convulsions, spikes of pleasure.

Then I finally felt his push, slow and careful, as my folds enveloped him, opening ever so wide to accommodate his massiveness. He took his time, remaining with just his tip inside me, giving slow shallow thrusts. A heavy hand ran up one leg to lay low on my abdomen, his thick thumb slipping down to press and caress my clit.

When Silence's lips next left mine, I whispered to him, "I want to suck on you, the way you did to Ant."

Surprise and a swell of desire flickered in his eyes as he shifted, kneeling beside me. My hand, already on his shaft, brought it to my mouth, and I created a seal with my lips, sucking gently upon him. His eyes rolled back, his hips rocking ever so slightly, thrusting into my mouth. One of his hands, on my breast, squeezed that soft, sensitive flesh, just as Ant pushed deeper within me. These two certainly knew how to work together — even though they couldn't have been doing it consciously — to bring me the most bliss. I rocked and shuddered with another orgasm, removing Silence's erection to gasp and moan before sucking upon him all the harder, as his moaning joined with mine.

With a slow, persistent push, Ant buried his monster erection deep inside me. He maintained his shallow thrusts, easy and slow, but still, the fullness of him, pressed so wonderfully tight inside my wet and sensitive sheath, was making me mad with pleasure, especially since his thumb was still stroking my clit.

"Silence, I'm going to shift," Ant said, his voice husky and low.

I let Silence withdraw from my lips, admiring the glistening tip of his manhood as he slid back a bit.

Ant put his hands under my sides and lifted me. I got the hint, wrapping my legs around him to help pull myself up. We met in a wet and hungry kiss as he turned around.

Then he was sitting on the bed. I unwrapped my legs and straddled him as he lay back, keeping his legs together. Silence got the hint and made a detour to my side-table —

for a refilled bottle of oil — before moving around behind me, also straddling Ant's legs.

I was in control now, at least where Ant was concerned. With all my weight upon him I keenly felt him pressing upon the deepest parts of me. His shaft pulsed and twitched in time with the beating of his heart. One of his hands reached down between us, his thumb once again pressing to my clit. He wasn't fully inside me, he was too big, a couple inches remaining outside. But I could lean forward a bit to press his thumb between us and put more pressure on my ragingly sensitive clit. Ant's other hand reached up to grasp a breast, massaging it with all the skill and power he'd used on my back earlier. Spirits, I loved how hard he was, insistent and grasping, just teasing the edges of pain.

I felt the cold touch of oil on my other opening, the press of Silence's fingers for a different type of massage. But I must have been quite ready for him as he didn't need to tease me open for very long before his slickened erection was pushing inside me. He grabbed my hips to pull me close, sinking deep into me.

I began a slow rocking motion, forward onto Ant, back onto Silence and the two of them joined the rhythm. Silence kissed my back and neck, one of his hands around me, low, slipping down to press on my clit, replacing Ant's. Ant brought his freed hand up to my other breast and now both were being gloriously, savagely, kneaded. I added more pressure still when I leaned forward, all my weight upon his hands.

I lost my breath as pleasure swept through me and spiraled up to wrap around my heart, squeezing every last drop of passion from me. I raised my hands up into my hair, playing and piling it, swaying and growing more frenzied in my movements upon the two hardened men. I was so ready, but wanted them to join me when I came.

"Please," I whispered. "Now!"

I shuddered with a full body wave of bliss, clenching tightly around both men, milking their lengths. I heard their corresponding grunts and moans. Ant swelled impossibly within me, and I knew his release was imminent as Silence found a new frenzied pace. For a moment, my orgasm jacked up to mind-blowing heights at the vigorous movement.

Then both men froze with final grunts and cries. There came an incredible pulsing flood, as both men exploded within me at once, sending me into a delirium of bliss as micro-orgasm after micro-orgasm built then blossomed into a massive tidal wave of pleasure surging through me. All we could do was twitch and groan for a long time, before we finally collapsed together in a sweaty heap of divinely satisfied bodies.

I was so loose from Ant's earlier massage and so extremely satisfied, that I dozed. I did indeed forget about my worries and the coming culmination of our plans, and when I woke to find both men cuddled close to me, somehow under the covers of my bed, I smiled and allowed myself to sleep again, relaxed and relieved. Hopefully I'd be ready for what was to come.

CHAPTER 18

THE VAUPHANI DELEGATION TO THE PEACE TALKS AND Monarchical Vote was led by Alvere. With him were Ahmaia, Eorthan, and Elvi of the Fey, a small honor guard of twelve of Vauphan's elite soldiers, and a contingent from Spider House.

Fin came, just in case we needed a quick exit. Other than that, I'd agonized over how many of my so-very-few people — my family — to bring.

Dove came, she'd insisted, even though I'd been unsure. She said her presence might help sway Silvermane, so I allowed it. Just in case though, I had Eorthan make her a set of armor like mine, only in gleaming silver over a gambeson of purest white. As with all things between us two sisters, she outshone me, seeming like some warrior goddess with her streaming blond hair and perfect poise. I wore my Fey armor as well, not taking any chances.

Sparrow stayed behind, since she was the only flying scout left at Cliffside with Dove gone. Silence and Ant insisted on coming to protect me. But to keep our party looking small, they remained in their avatar forms in a special pouch at my belt, ready to pop out at a moment's notice. Midnight was around somewhere, unseen as usual.

The final member of our party was my "special guest" Lord War, currently travelling in one of Ahmaia's pouches.

Ursa wasn't with us, she'd returned to Grizzly house as their second and would arrive with that delegation.

As I marched down the main avenue of Miraline I saw my parents waving from the side of the street. They looked concerned. If they'd heard any of the rumors floating around about me or Dove, I didn't blame them. I waved back, as did Dove, but we couldn't speak to them, not yet. We were part of a formal delegation and stayed with our host, the King of Vauphan. Alvere looked truly Royal that day, in a cloak of deepest purple lined in ermine. His clothes beneath were of navy and gold. His Black hair was free, flowing down to his shoulders, glistening blue-white in the late spring sun. Those beryl-blue eyes were focused ahead, on The Great Hall of Miraline, one of the three largest buildings in the city. The other two were the mayor's manor and the library, all of which were on the grounds of the mayor's estate. Those buildings had all been emptied, which was why my parents weren't at their books today.

We entered through the large double-doors and were shown to our section of the hall. There was but a single chair, for Alvere, the rest of us were meant to stand near or behind him.

We were not the first to arrive. Merlin was there, Hale at her side as her new second. Swan stood amongst the Owl House delegation, along with over a score of others. She glared at me.

I smiled back easily. And when I caught Hale's eye, my smile only grew, though it wasn't with mirth. I was thinking about squashing him like a bug.

Others already in attendance included Fang and Retriever of House Pterolycus, with a score of their Nobles. Fang looked just as menacing as usual, big and dark and powerful, glaring at everyone, not just me. Retriever's golden eyes scanned over everyone present. I couldn't read that hard look. She didn't seem impressed with me, but then... she didn't seem impressed with anyone else either.

The only other Noble present I didn't recognize. They were seated beside Merlin with only a very small contingent behind them of two others, that was it. By process of elimination I figured this had to be the representative of House Panther. The woman seemed small and fidgety, as if she wanted to run from this meeting. I got the feeling it was fear and awe of Merlin that kept her here.

The others arrived in short order. Spike and his second Quill of house Porcupine. Quill was Spike's brother, and his avatar was actually a hedgehog, but the two men looked so similar most people just assumed they shared the same avatar.

Skyfire and Silvermane arrived together, talking quietly. I found that intensely intriguing but couldn't do much about it. I couldn't quite hear them either. My spider senses were on high alert, but there was too much other chatter in the hall and the two women were speaking far too softly. Behind them Drake and Horn entered, both tall, but otherwise vastly different, Horn was large and fair with greying hair. Drake was thin and dark, but still exuded presence and power. The two men didn't talk to each other. It was as if there were some unseen barrier between them, that's how 'cold' they seemed to each other.

Lady Tanuki and her second Red arrived next, both willowy and tall, genuinely happy to see everyone. Their House seemed so... happy. I envied them just a little.

Last to arrive was Grizzly and Ursa with a small contingent, which made sense since they'd have come the farthest to get here. Grizzly didn't look at anyone really, just seemed vaguely dangerous as he took his seat. Ursa stood next to him. She didn't acknowledge me. We had to keep our association a secret, for now.

And then... we began.

"We call this Council of Nobles to order," Merlin called out in a clear voice. I couldn't help but grimace at her usage of the royal "we." Queen Whitewing had never used it. "Our beloved queen was slain by a betrayer, and a new king or queen must be selected. We also have, as our special guest, the King of Vauphan, who has seen the might of Elista and wishes to sue for peace."

That was interesting wording. It definitely made it sound like Elista had the upper hand, when in truth the war was a stalemate at the moment.

"The King offers his hand in marriage should we choose a queen. And if we should choose a king, his daughter shall marry our king's first son."

Wait what? Daughter...? Why had she not said 'children?' Why so specific?

Do you think she knows? Auwei asked.

How could she? Unless... she's the one who's seen the future?

That sent just a bit of a chill through me.

Less than a week ago, Auwei, with her intimate connection to my body, had informed me I was pregnant... with a girl... Alvere's child. This child wouldn't be recognized by Vauphan as a legal offspring of the King of course, but still...

I couldn't help but put a hand to my stomach. The inadvertent reaction of my armor was to peel away, allowing me access to my spider-silk. Many eyes in the room caught the movement, and I quickly put my hand at my side once more. That had been a mistake.

Merlin continued, "Since this is a time of war, we wish to invoke the seventh codex, which states that the current ruling house will remain in power during times of war, even if the king or queen is killed. Their second shall take their place until such time as the war is concluded."

"And the war is concluded," Skyfire said quickly. "The king's presence here is indication enough of that. I do not accept your invocation."

That caused a few murmurs around the room. Still the new head of House Panther seconded the motion and a vote was held, but no other Nobles voted in favor.

I was a little surprised by this.

Auwei, as always, was there to help me understand. *This doesn't mean the others don't want Merlin to be queen, it only means they are agreeing with Skyfire that the war is concluded and the seventh codex won't be a factor. It means they want to hear arguments for and against certain members first, before they make their choice for monarch. Even if there are those who are already on Merlin's side it behooves them to vote against this, so as to look impartial when they vote for the next monarch.*

That made sense.

"Then we shall hear nominations and arguments," Merlin said, smiling just a little too contentedly. She thought this was all going according to her plan. I certainly hoped that wouldn't be the case.

Almost before Merlin had stopped speaking, the new House Panther leader spoke up in a tremulous voice. "I nominate Merlin of House Owl!"

There were a few chuckles in the room.

Auwei assisted me again. *She spoke out of turn. The first step in any meeting like this is always for each House Leader to re-introduce themselves and THEN state any nominations. As a new House Leader, she would undoubtedly go last. Merlin should speak first.*

Merlin smiled. "Thank you, Lady Margay," Merlin said as she rose. "I am Lady Merlin of House Owl. First, with the leader of my house recently deceased comes the choice of a new name for my House. I choose to respect our previous and illustrious queen and keep House Owl."

A bold move, not claiming the House title for herself. It makes her look modest, though perhaps weak as well. Interesting. Auwei was quite caught up in all this intrigue. I just wanted to survive today and come out of this with a new king or queen, I didn't much care who, just not Merlin.

"As the new leader of House Owl, we formally denounce house Maverick and the so-called successor House Spider. We seek to remove them from the lists of Nobles. We also nominate ourselves for the next queen. House Owl has ruled well for thirty years and we know We can continue that noble tradition." She looked over at Alvere, her gaze sliding over me. She smiled, but her expression bore no kindness, just... possession and greed. "We will happily marry King Alvere and produce for him an heir who would rule our combined kingdoms." She sat again slowly, gracefully. She didn't even offer arguments for why she should be queen. That's how confident she was that she'd already won this battle.

We'd see.

Skyfire rose next. "I am Lady Skyfire of House Wyvern." She stepped forward into the roughly circular open space in the middle of the room and took a long moment to look around at each Noble. What I found most interesting was how she included me in that group. Her gaze held mine for a long moment, not Alvere's, mine. That was a quiet nod to my right to be a House Leader, very interesting indeed. When she spoke, her voice was hot and impassioned, as usual. "I see no solid proof of the betrayal of House Maverick and its successor House Spider," she said, voice carrying. "I have heard rumors and hearsay, but no proof has been presented to me. So, upon the question of removing House Spider from the lists I delay my vote. If any here has evidence to present. Do so."

Well, that wasn't a huge vote of confidence, just a delay. But it was something.

"On the question of the new monarch..." Skyfire paused, holding the room's attention in her palm and milking every moment of silence. "I nominate Lady Silvermane of House Pegasus."

The room murmured for a long moment at this. Silvermane, despite having a powerful house, was still one of the younger and newer leaders. She wasn't even thirty, and her house was only eight years old. Compared to some of the others that made her very inexperienced.

That's a surprise, I was sure she'd vote for herself. Auwei was a little aghast.

When we asked, she said she didn't want to be queen. She's a powerful woman, but she likes her position.

True.

The murmuring died down, and Skyfire continued, "Silvermane may be one of the younger leaders, and of a newer House, but—" She drove her finger up into the air to emphasize her coming point. "In the short time that Pegasus House has existed, Lady Silvermane has made it a powerful and indomitable force in Elista. If nothing else, this proves her worthiness to rule. I believe she will be a fair and equitable queen and a handsome bride for King Alvere."

I looked at Lord Horn. He wasn't happy. I didn't blame

him. I was in his same position, lover to someone who might potentially soon marry another.

Interesting. Auwei said drawing the word out.

What? I asked.

I... don't know yet. And I don't want to say anything until I'm more certain.

Fine, be all mysterious and stubborn like that.

Fine... I will.

"That is all I have to say," Skyfire said, bowing to the assembly with a flourish. She then returned to her chair. Spirits, she was always so dynamic in everything she did. I couldn't help but admire her. I was ready to vote for Silvermane, even if that meant handing Alvere over to the woman. Though, we'd see if I'd even have a vote at all in any of this.

Fang rose.

I didn't know much of the man, but everything I'd heard was that he had some odd affectations and was generally a man of few words.

"Fang votes to remove House Spider. Fang votes for Merlin." He sat again.

"I'm curious Fangy," Skyfire said, out of turn, but not caring at all. "Do you have any evidence against House Spider?"

Fang looked to Retriever who stepped forward. She looked at me directly. "We have it on good authority that Legs kidnapped and killed the queen. Do you deny this?" she asked me directly.

"For the charge of kidnapping, I do not deny it," I said, loud and proud. I'd done it and I'd face any consequences for it. "For the charge of killing the queen, yes, I deny it." I said no more. That was as it should be. If asked, I could go on, but otherwise I should keep any out-of-turn speaking to a minimum.

A murmur rose in the hall and quickly died down as Retriever held up her hand. "And do you deny killing Lady Claw of House Panther, or that members of your house killed Jaguar, Tiger, Lynx, and Lion of House Panther? Do you deny working with the Vauphani against us in the war?"

That was a bit harder to answer. I tried not to smile, thinking about my revenge upon Lady Claw. In truth, that hadn't brought me the satisfaction I'd hoped.

Oddly, before I could answer, it was Skyfire who came to my rescue, sort of. "That was war, Puppy." Retriever glared at Skyfire, clearly not liking that nickname. "And yes, Legs may have been on the other side, but who's to say she wasn't trying to make peace? Things get confusing in war."

"Members of House Panther saw Legs kill Lady Claw at night, during a sneak attack!" Retriever growled, growing angrier.

"After we attacked the Vauphani at night, in a sneak attack, isn't that right?" Skyfire asked easily.

Several people gasped and low murmurs filled the hall. That was clearly not common knowledge.

"It was, yes," Retriever said sourly.

"Then, like I said. War is war. The girl has admitted to kidnapping the queen, and that's going to have consequences. but we can't know for certain how the queen died or by whose hand, *unless*... anyone has a way to be certain?" Skyfire looked around. It was a testament to her guile that she didn't look in Ursa's direction at all.

"If I may!" Ursa spoke up stepping forward. "I have a spirit-gift which allows me to know a person's mind, I can sense truth. Shall I use it?"

As far as I knew, no one other than Silvermane and Skyfire knew Ursa and I had been working together. The murmurs around the hall died down as Retriever smiled. "Yes, that would be wonderful, thank you Lady Ursa." She motioned to me.

Ursa crossed the floor to stand before me. She addressed me harshly, directly.

"Lady Legs, did you or did you not kidnap the queen?"

"I did."

"Truth!" Ursa looked around before going on. "Did you kill the queen?"

"I did not."

"Truth!" That got a wave of chatter. Merlin's brow furrowed, her face dark with rage. Ursa waited for the hubbub to die down then asked. "Did anyone in your House kill the queen?"

"No."

"Truth!" More chatter. Again, Ursa waited then asked, "How did the queen die?"

"After we took her to our home, simply to ask her a few questions, she began to have trouble breathing. She did not seem to be able to get air. She suffocated and after she died a puff of mist came from her mouth. I cannot be certain, but I believe she was under the curse of a mistweaver."

That got the place into a full-on uproar. Shouts of "liar" and "mistweavers aren't real" dominated the calls.

Ursa waited. "Lady Legs' description of the queen's death is truth. And though it is truth that Legs *believes* the death was caused by a mistweaver, that is conjecture only." She turned to me with a vague wave of dismissal. "Unless you have proof a mistweaver exists?"

"I do, or rather, one did, before I killed her."

Ursa gave a masterfully shocked reaction, then shouted,

"This is truth! A mistweaver did exist, and Lady Legs killed her!"

That sent the hall into a shocked silence.

Going on quickly, Ursa asked, "Sometimes, before a person dies, they implicate who they think caused their death. Did the queen give you any name before she died?"

Oh... another masterfully asked question. Ursa knew as well as I did that the queen's mention of Merlin was vague and unfinished, but by asking only if a name was mentioned it was easy for me to say:

"Yes, she said one name: Merlin."

CHAPTER 19

MERLIN FLEW FROM HER CHAIR AND SHOUTED. "THAT'S A LIE!" Spittle flew from her lips. She was so vehement everyone in the room jerked back with alarm, including me.

Ursa turned slowly. "No, it is truth. The queen spoke your name." Ursa, living dangerously, approached Lady Merlin. "Tell me, Lady Merlin, were you aware that a mist-weaver existed?"

Merlin was barely holding on. "No!"

"That..." Ursa said slowly, with masterfully acted confusion and shock, "is a lie."

Merlin glared daggers at Ursa. Hale stepped in and restrained the small woman before she threw herself bodily at Ursa, which seemed likely to be her next move. "How could you? I trusted you," Merlin spat.

The rest of the hall, recovered from Merlin's outburst, was in an uproar once again. And happily, for the first time, it wasn't my fault.

With momentum moving in my favor, I decided now was the best time to spring my little surprise.

"Lady Ursa!" I called out over the raised voices of concern and confusion in the hall. "Would you mind questioning another I've brought along?" I turned and nodded to Ahmaia.

A moment later Lord War was standing in the hall, not far from me and looking very angry.

I couldn't help a smile as more voices around the hall joined the confused cacophony.

"I believe he knows more about this war then most here have been told," I shouted over the tumult of voices.

Ursa nodded and approached the seething warlord. Lord War glared at her. The best part of all of this was that he wouldn't know she could tell truth and lies. He'd not known anything which had happened up until now. Ahmaia had made sure he could hear none of what had gone on.

Ursa asked simply: "Lord War, before the gathered Nobles here, would you tell us how the war began?"

War scoffed and grinned. "Gladly. The war began when Vauphan threatened our northern borders. Our spies informed us they intended to invade and capture our Mists!" He'd raised his voice, even though the gathered Nobles had begun to hush to hear him.

"That is a lie," Ursa said evenly and sounding just a bit curious.

"It is not!" Lord War, even though shackled, bunched his muscles as if he intended to strike her.

A roar rocked the hall, which silenced everyone and froze them in place. It hadn't been Ursa, but Grizzly himself, who'd veered into his massive, fearsome bear form. He shifted back quickly. "Lord War! Perhaps you are unaware, but my second has the ability to discern truth from lies. If she says you lie, then you are questioning the veracity and loyalty of Ursa, myself, and my House!" The challenge was implicit, but Lord Grizzly made it very clear. "If you deny the truth once more, you'll face me in a Noble's Duel!"

Lord War did not look afraid in the least, almost... interested. He was certain of his abilities and his strength. He grinned, even let out a laugh. "I might like that, Lord Grizzly. Don't tempt me."

"I think it's time the truth was made known." This, surprisingly came from Lord Horn. The large man in silvery armor, with grey dominating his beard and hair, stepped forward.

Silvermane looked surprised.

I glanced over at Hale, who looked just a little panicked.

Horn stepped forward to the center of the circle, glaring at Lord War. It was clear those two didn't much like each other. "I have kept this secret from even my own mistress." He turned to Silvermane. "I'm sorry," he said, ashamed. "My son convinced me it was for the best of the nation, for all of Elista, but if it is, then all of Elista should know it."

A hush fell over the hall. Everyone listened intently.

"The war was no contrivance of Vauphan." Horn's voice was clear and carried. "We invaded, quietly at first, slowly taking farmers' lands. This began over three years ago. We began this war."

That caused a hubbub, and it was interesting to see who the chatter was coming from. Mostly it was lesser Nobles. It was clear Lord Fang knew the truth. He didn't seem surprised at all. Grizzly and Skyfire didn't seem shocked either, but we'd already told them the truth. Tanuki and Spike were clearly surprised. Silvermane was shocked, though it was hard to tell from what: the news of the war, or her lover having betrayed her.

"And the reason we did so was to protect our Mists,"

Horn said slowly. "It was discovered not long ago, that the Mists are moving, and within a few generations they won't even be in Elista any longer. We sought only to protect our heritage." He turned to Alvere. "I am sorry for our treachery, Your Majesty."

Alvere nodded. "Thank you for your honesty, Lord Horn."

No one even looked to Ursa to verify if this was the truth. By this point, we all knew it.

"We have to remain strong!" Merlin shouted, drawing everyone's attention to her. She had regained herself *a little* from her earlier outburst, seeming to vibrate with a barely restrained, trembling intensity. She turned to Alvere. "Would you have let us cross your borders to visit our Mists?"

"Perhaps," Alvere said evenly. "We have had peace for many years before this. The Vauphani do not want your Mists. It is clear that they are a part of your cultural heritage and you would have been welcome to continue your traditions."

Merlin seemed a bit shocked at that. But she quickly countered with, "Ah! But you would not be King forever, and by the time the Mists are within your lands, the King of that time may not allow us in!"

"And that justified war and death?" Alvere countered evenly.

"Yes!" Merlin shouted before she realized what she'd said. She calmed quickly. She twisted her face to a strained-looking, odd, contorted semblance of peace. "I call for the vote now! Let's settle this and make the peace this King has promised! Who votes for me?" she shouted. "Raise your hands!"

This was breaking all sorts of protocol, but given all the

other disruptions to the meeting people seemed to go with it. Merlin herself raised her hand, as did Fang; it was clear he was in her pocket. Not surprisingly Margay, the puppet leader of House Panther, also raised her hand. That was it.

Merlin's eyes bulged with rage. "Traitors!" she shouted.

"Who votes for Lady Silvermane?" Skyfire shouted, raising her hand. Grizzly and Spike joined her. Oddly that was it. I found it odd Lady Silvermane didn't vote for herself. Everyone looked at her.

"I am curious who Lady Tanuki votes for?" Silvermane said softly.

Tanuki accepted the looks from everyone in the room with a cool smile. "This is a momentous occasion, and I do not believe this choice should be made lightly." She looked over at me. "Also, we have not determined the validity of Lady Legs' House and whether she has a vote. So, I abstain for now. Too much remains uncertain."

"Legs is a traitor!" Merlin seethed. "She gets no vote!"

"That has not been definitively determined," Tanuki countered.

Merlin glared at the Noblewoman. "You're a traitor too!"

"Because I will not vote for you?"

"Yes!" Merlin's tenuous façade was breaking down, her madness starting to show through.

Time for me to push her over the edge.

I stepped forward. The space in the center of the hall was getting a little crowded with the large Lord Horn, the dangerous Lord War, and the powerful presence of Lady Ursa, and now me.

I felt my *Hero* gift rise within me as I spoke. "Let Lady Ursa vouch for the truth of my words!" And whether it was my gift or the power alone in my voice, the hall hushed.

"Lady Silvermane, though it would pain both of us, I believe you would make a far better queen than Lady Merlin. I urge you to vote for yourself, bring stability and peace back to our torn nation!" With Tanuki abstaining, it fell only to Lady Silvermane to vote. If she voted for herself this would all be over. "I will submit to whatever punishment you deem necessary for my actions against your mother, the queen. Though it has been attested that I did not kill her. I believe that to be the work of the mistweaver, whom I have already dealt with. So, in a way I have already killed your mother's killer."

Something caught my eye then, it was subtle and only there for a moment, but I was certain I saw two quick emotions flash over Merlin's face at my words. She'd seemed furious at the mention of my killing the mistweaver, then... oddly satisfied and relieved at the mention of the queen's killer being brought to justice. Very odd indeed.

I addressed the hall next. "We have become a divided nation, at war with ourselves and our neighbors. We need to be united and strong. If that means the dissolution of my House, I am willing to do that. But I ask you to look around and ask yourselves. Would you be so willing? If it was for the best of our beloved Elista, would you give away your power and dissolve your House? If we are not willing to do that, then we have lost our way. We should be servants of the people, not despots addicted to power. So punish me if you will, remove my House from the lists, but do so only in a nation that is united in peace and only when you have taken a long look at your own House!"

"Wise words," Ursa said. Her words carried to all corners of the hall. She turned to Silvermane. "Lady? How do you vote?"

Silvermane looked pensive, sturdier than she had before, when she'd learned Horn had been lying to her, but still undecided.

"My Lady?" Dove stepped forward and all eyes turned to her. She was a picture of strength and beauty in her silver armor, those blue eyes flashing with courage. I was certain no one in the hall would be able to look away from her. "I was once of your House, and would return, if you will have me. I fled because Lord Hale attacked me." She looked briefly at the large man. He didn't even try to deny it, glaring at Dove with lustful superiority on his face. He didn't think his house would fall.

"This is truth," Ursa said, resolute.

"Indeed," Dove continued. "He got close to me, only to attack and try to kill my sister. It was that which drove her into hiding and also when she began to suspect there was rot within the Royal House. I will not say anymore as to whom I suspect is behind Lord Hale's actions. I say only this: you, Lady Silvermane would make a far better replacement for your mother than any other here. I urge you to vote for yourself and end this madness."

Lady Silvermane took a long look at Dove, nodding, then slowly looked around the room. "Indeed," she said to herself, then drew herself up and spoke. "I vote for myse—"

Time seemed to slow.

I caught movement from the corner of my eye: Merlin raising her arms. Mists spilled out from her palms forming two massive blades in front of her outstretched hands. One she unleased toward Lady Silvermane. The second came for me.

I knew, from my encounter with her, that Lady Skyfire could move with incredible speed and she did so then, sprinting like a blur to block the blow meant for Silvermane. The massive mist-blade severed her left arm mid-bicep and bit deeply into the left side of her chest. Even with that sacrifice she didn't block it fully and the blade took Silvermane low on her torso, throwing her back against the wall behind her, and pinning her there, blood gushing out of her from the hole in her abdomen.

My mind whirled with the realization that Merlin was a mistweaver, even as I tried to throw myself out of the way of the mist-blade meant for me. I was too slow.

Someone pushed me down. The blade only just clipped my right arm, but it hit my savior — Dove, my beloved sister — on the left side of her chest, spinning her around with a wild spray of blood as she screamed and fell to the floor, limp.

Time resumed.

Chaos erupted. People screamed and ran.

"Ant!" I shouted, though my voice didn't seem to be making a dent in the uproar. "Come out. Save..." He was there, standing next to me, but words had stalled on my tongue. Dove was closer and probably not as badly injured as Silvermane. And if Silvermane was to be the next queen. Spirits, it was a horrible choice. I felt hot tears on my cheek as I said. "Silvermane. Save Silvermane!"

He nodded and began pushing through the chaos of Nobles.

I spun out a glob of spider-silk into my hand and slapped it onto my arm as I crawled over to Dove.

Merlin, floating high above the commotion, on a cushion of mist, laughed maniacally, throwing more razor-sharp bolts of mist toward the Nobles who had voted against her.

"Pits Below! She's a mistweaver?" Silence said next to me, having come out of his avatar form.

Ah... yeah!

And suddenly I understood those strange looks of hers from a moment before. I'd said I'd killed the queen's killer, but I hadn't. I was certain now...

...Merlin had cursed the queen.

CHAPTER 20

People ran in all directions, screaming and panicked.

My arm stung like an over-sized paper-cut, but I'd stopped the bleeding with my spider-silk.

Silence tried to help me up, but I pushed him away as I reached Dove.

"I'm not the one that needs help, can you do anything for her?" There was so much blood around my sister, staining that white gambeson a garish red. I clamped a wad of spider-silk over her wound, but it wasn't enough. She kept bleeding.

"I'll do what I can," Silence said kneeling next to her as I doled out more spider silk. He tore off his shirt and pressed it to her wound. That seemed to help... a little.

I rose and took in the scene. My eye caught Ahmaia's. She'd been headed for Alvere, but, seeing my desperate look, she glanced at Dove and nodded. I wasn't sure what she could do, but she hurried over and a moment later long strands of cloth were tightly binding the deep wound.

Good.

The hall was in complete chaos. Hale and the Nobles of Owl House were openly fighting other Nobles. Fang was on their side, despite being across the hall from them. The battle was hindering Ant from getting to Silvermane, but Horn and Skyfire were already at the woman. I didn't know what they could do, and Skyfire herself was in bad shape, but they seemed to be trying to help her. So I turned my attention to Merlin, still hovering high enough to be out of reach of anyone in the hall, laughing as she sowed destruction around her.

My *Hero* gift surged, and suddenly the pain in my arm wasn't as intense. I hadn't thought I'd be able to wield a weapon, but now...

Drawing my sword, I leaped, easily reaching her and slashing with my blade. I needed to end this now. I'd done what I'd come to do, expose Merlin for the villain she was... though now I could see how devastating that discovery had been for the others present. This madness was — as usual — my fault, and I needed to end it. I'd killed one mist-weaver, so why not two?

With an easy laugh, Merlin waved a hand and a shield of mist blocked my blow. Then, that same shield, hard as steel, slammed into me, throwing me back, pressed to a wall, constricting around me. The binding mists compressed my chest, my arms held tight at my side. Without my Fey armor, I'd have several broken ribs right now. As it was, I couldn't quite catch my breath.

Merlin flashed from where she was in a puff of Mist and appeared next to me.

"I don't think I'll kill you now," she said, in a low venomous tone, madness and vengeance in her eyes. "But you need to pay for killing my sister, Hazra."

Her sister? The other mistweaver had been her sister? Now the pained look on her face when I'd mentioned killing the mistweaver made sense.

Spikes slowly speared into me from the mist clamping me to the wall. My armor stopped most of them, but where my armor didn't cover, my neck, and hands and the small gaps between the plates, pain burned through my skin. I gritted my teeth, not wishing to give her the pleasure of hearing me scream. But she could clearly see I was in pain.

"Oh, yes, that is delicious, but not the sort of pain I wish you to feel. No, you need to feel the pain of loss, of losing someone you care for deeply." She swung her head around looking at those in my party. "Your sister perhaps?" she said. "That is fitting, yes. But she is already dying." She swung her gaze back to me. "But you need to suffer so much more than I did. Twice as much perhaps? Shall I take another from you?" Her head swung around again and locked on Alvere. "The King perhaps? You love him, do you not?"

"No!" I couldn't help it. The word escaped my lips before I could stop it.

She chuckled. "Yes, that would be perfect. A sister and a lover." Her gaze returned to me. "I'll cripple your body so you'll no longer be a threat and take those you love from you." She laughed. "That is what you get for working against me, little one."

The mists around me crushed harder, spikes digging deeper. I felt the bones in my arms crack, heard the hollow popping sounds. My ribs would give way next. Even my armor, strong as it was, couldn't stop this force.

Merlin laughed as she flashed away in a swirl of mist to arrive next to Alvere, who was up and had his sword out, his honor-guard creating a circle around him. But they were facing out and never saw Merlin grasp his neck and lift him from the ground. She looked back at me as she choked him, his sword falling from his spasming hand as he flailed against her. She circled slowly so she could keep eye-contact with me as she brought Alvere's face to hers in a mock kiss. Mist flowed from her mouth into his and the spasming stopped suddenly.

She grinned, then vanished, disappearing with Alvere, both gone.

No! I tried to scream, but I had no air. I struggled to breathe as pain surged through me. Ribs fractured and cracked with a new surge of pain. As hard as I struggled to hold on, to hold out, to fight against this magic, I couldn't. My breath wouldn't come. The world faded away to darkness, an inky nothingness filled with pain and loss.

I'd enraged Merlin, and it had backfired horribly.

I knew I wouldn't die, not yet, she'd promised that. But as I succumbed to unconsciousness, I also knew... I'd lost this fight.

I woke with a gasp. My eyes snapped open to see the haggard and exhausted face of Ant above me.

"Oh, thank the Spirits," he breathed.

I still felt a burning agony over so much of me, but my breathing came easier, my ribs no longer pained. He must have thought me dead, but I knew better. That had not been Merlin's plan. Though I doubt Merlin's plan had included Ant healing me either.

Still, even though my body was mending, my soul was shattered.

"Alvere," I breathed the name, voice hoarse. "Dove."

"I stabilized Dove, but she'd lost a lot of blood. I don't know if she'll pull through. I'm sorry Legs. The same is true of Lady Silvermane. She's been taken to other healers as we speak, alive for now." He swallowed hard. "But... Alvere is missing."

No! My soul clenched in a new agony.

I could do so little in that moment, lying on my back in the hall. The fighting seemed to have stopped, but I didn't really care about that. My heart burned with an indomitable ache for my sister and Alvere, so I simply wept.

"I'm sorry," Ant said softly. "I... I need to go, others are hurt." I heard him rise and the heavy footfalls moving away.

But a moment later, lighter ones drew near. "Oh, Blessed Spirits! Legs!" Silence's voice. A soft hand touched my cheek, one of the few spots that didn't still hurt. I opened my eyes, but couldn't speak, voice choked with the sobs I couldn't stop.

Silence leaned down, careful not to touch certain parts of me — I guess I looked as bad as I felt — and pressed my face to his chest in an awkward embrace.

"They'll survive," he said softly. "And we'll get Alvere back, don't you worry."

If he wasn't already dead. He'd been hanging so limp and lifeless in Merlin's grip. And even if he wasn't dead, perhaps the mists she'd forced into him were a curse like the queen's? If we rescued him, it might just mean his death.

"Just rest for now," Silence said. "The fighting's over. We need to regroup and recover. Then we can make Merlin pay for what she's done."

He was right.

I felt my *Hero* gift surge within me, helping to numb the agony as I rose. My tears stopped as my jaw tightened.

Silence held me closer, a bit easier now that I was sitting.

And in that moment, even though I still couldn't speak, I vowed to all the Spirits and any gods that might listen, that I would kill Merlin and make her pay for what had happened here. She'd made a mistake, leaving me alive, a dire one, and I intended to make her realize the full and vicious depths of that mistake before she died.

CHAPTER 21

DESPITE MY VOW OF VENGEANCE, NOTHING HAPPENED RIGHT away. We remained in Miraline for nearly another week as people recovered. With my gift, I was well by the third day. Even though I told him not to, Ant visited often to give me what little energy he had, looking more and more worn out. Dove healed, but remained in a prolonged sleep of recovery, still and pale. My parents took Dove to their residence to rest, in their care. I told them both I was so sorry for what had happened. They didn't blame me, but I did. Fin visited her often and got to know my parents. They were overjoyed that Dove had met a good man.

We got word that Lady Silvermane would live, though it would take her a long time to fully recover.

A few other Nobles had been seriously hurt, but not any of the House Leaders, except Lady Skyfire. She was a tough one though, up and about soon enough, despite orders to rest.

That left Grizzly as well as Lady Tanuki and Lord Spike as the full Noble's Council for the moment.

As for our foes? Unfortunately, Lord Hale and Lady

Swan escaped. Though much of the rest of House Owl had been captured or killed in the fight. Lord Fang was dead and Lady Retriever was being held in custody, as was most of the Pterolycus House. Lady Margay of House Panther had survived and surrendered. She was cooperating now, telling the others everything she knew, which unfortunately wasn't much.

On the fourth day after the event, I was called before the reduced Noble's Council.

Lord Drake was there, to represent House Wyvern, even though he'd have no vote. A woman I didn't recognize represented House Pegasus. They were arranged in a line across one side of the hall, the three heads of Houses sitting, while everyone else stood. I was happy to see Lady Ursa alive and well, though also bandaged, her left arm in a sling.

"Lady Legs," Grizzly said, then shook his head. "That name of yours is... interesting." The large man was still covered in bandages, but they didn't seem to hamper him.

"I know, and I have to live with it," I said with a grimace.

He nodded. "You have been called before *what's left* of the Noble's Council for a reckoning."

I nodded. "I accept that the events of the peace talks were my doing," I said stoically. "I was the one who arranged it and who, in many ways, urged Merlin to madness. I am deeply sorry for—"

"Shut up and let me talk, woman!" Grizzly growled.

So... I did.

"No one here blames you for those events." He sighed heavily. "I can see how you might blame yourself, but you'll need to stop that if you're to lead your House effectively."

Did you hear that? Auwei said, enthusiastically. She was trying to lift my spirits after everything that had happened.

But what does that mean? Lead my House? Have they accepted me?

I think so.

I didn't ask Grizzly though. He'd told me to shut up. So I remained silent, for now.

Grizzly continued. "Through *various* means, we have ascertained the events of the past few months. We even have a clearer picture of what happened over the past three years, since the war began. The war is definitely *not* your fault, and if it hadn't been for you, none of us would know the truth of what Merlin had been doing. We know you are no traitor to the Crown, so your standing as head of House Spider is affirmed. Welcome to the Council of Nobles."

See, I knew you'd be exonerated!

They're not done yet. I still have to account for kidnapping the queen.

"Thank you, my Lord," I said with a bow. Even though I was technically his equal as a House Head, I was still of a junior House and owed him respect for his seniority and experience.

"Now," he said, gruff and stern.

And here it comes...

"You killed a mistweaver once, any idea how to deal with Merlin?"

That was not what I'd expected. Apparently, we were going to skip over the queen-napping for now and move on to other matters.

I must have been shocked for a moment too long as Grizzly then prompted me with: "You can speak now."

I found my words. "I will personally kill Merlin and Lord Hale," I said with a vicious grin. "She's plagued this nation long enough and she..." I swallowed hard. I could say it. "She killed—"

"The King of Vauphan is alive," Ursa said firmly.

The force of those words nearly knocked me over.

"What?"

"King Alvere is alive. We got word from the capital that Merlin is holding him for ransom. She'll return him to Vauphan once we and the Vauphani recognize her as queen... of both countries."

"Bloody Pits!" I couldn't help myself.

Grizzly gave a significant look to Ursa. Ursa's look was just as cool. "She needed to know."

"You weren't going to tell me?" I blurted.

"We didn't want you running off before we'd had a chance to determine our course of action."

"And if it were your wife, someone you loved, would *you* wait?" I shot back.

Grizzly grumbled. It was clear he'd not want to wait either. "From what I hear you have many 'loves.'"

Really? That was his argument. You have others...?

I didn't want to shout at him, so I took a moment to calm myself. I answered with, "Don't we all have many people we love, who we'd die for, who we'd want to rescue from madmen or madwomen?" I knew he was sleeping with not only Ursa, but also Blackclaw. I was sure he loved more than one person himself.

He grumbled again. "And what do you plan to do, knowing this?"

I very much wanted to run off and save Alvere immediately. But... "I will wait and see what this Council decides," I said diplomatically.

"And if you don't like it, you'll do your own thing?" Lady Tanuki said with a faint grin.

I looked at the calm visage of the astute woman and nodded. "Pretty much, yes."

She sighed. "Oh, to be young again."

"There is more," Ursa said with a heavy sigh. "From what we've heard, the Vauphani nobles are strongly considering ignoring Merlin and... raising a new king from their own ranks. Apparently, they were not happy with Alvere's short reign as king. He'd talked about doing away with the nobility. This way they can keep their titles and get rid of a nuisance."

"But..." Wow, just wow. "That will infuriate Merlin. She'll kill Alvere!"

"Exactly." Grizzly grumbled. "That way the blood isn't on the hands of those sniveling *hereditary* nobles."

This wasn't good at all. "So, what's your plan?" I asked.

The assembled Nobles looked at each other. It was clear they had all been thinking about this but not decided anything.

"We were waiting for you," Grizzly said stoically.

And in that moment, it became clear to me that despite the many years of experience of the lords and ladies gathered in this room, they had no clue how to deal with a situation like this. All they'd ever done was debate minor changes to government and protect their lands.

But I'd been battling mistweavers and dealing with internal intrigue for nearly all of my — admittedly short — Noble career.

In this matter, I had far more experience than they did.

But before we got any further there was one thing — a curiosity that had been driving me mad — I wanted to know. I turned to Lord Drake and asked him directly, "You have a spirit-gift, yes? What is it?"

Everyone looked at him.

"Apparently my secret is out." He grimaced, his dark eyes drilling into me. Then he sighed. "But yes, perhaps it is wise for us to share our various gifts if they might be of use in what is to come. I, as Lady Legs knows, can see things others cannot. I see people's auras and can often determine how they feel by seeing even the slightest change in their expressions and carriage."

So that was it.

Grizzly shared that he had a gift of strength, making him far stronger than he should be. But none of the others had any gifts. I told them of my *Hero* gift, and we moved on to planning how to defeat Merlin.

"Can I get a chair?" I asked. "I think we're going to be here for a while."

And at that, several of the others visibly relaxed. For all of their seniority over me, I'd just taken control of this meeting... and that had been exactly what they'd wanted.

Didn't I say you were destined for great things? Auwei said with pride.

I don't know if you ever used those words exactly, but... thank you for your faith in me.

As you can see now, it was well deserved.

Indeed.

By the end of the afternoon, we had a plan, if a rough one. And even though every fiber of my being was yelling at me to run and save Alvere, I knew I had to stay here and oversee this new, small coalition. They all deferred to me, even Grizzly. He was big and tough and in a one-on-one fight I'd not want to face him, but strategizing an internal coup... was not his forte.

Apparently, it was mine.

Merlin held the capital and had the considerable might of the Owl House army protecting her, not to mention the city's defenses. A frontal assault would only harm citizens and weaken our armies as a whole. So, the plan was to assemble the rest of the combined armies and march on the capital in a show of force, but go no further than Elismount, a wide hill overlooking the city from the north. We'd stop and dig in there and see if Merlin sent her forces out to meet us. That way there would be no fighting inside the city.

But the hope was to avoid that fight with subterfuge. From my House's scouting, we knew of a secret way into the Owl House residence by means of a tavern called The Slippery Eel. And, from questioning one of the House Owl captives, we now knew the exact route through the warren of tunnels to get into the estate.

The plan was simple, a small group would sneak into the city and through those tunnels into the residence. We'd free Alvere first, making sure he was safe, then face Merlin.

As much as Merlin and Hale were on my list and I'd sworn to kill both of them, the other Nobles convinced me that they should be captured, if possible, to be tried for treason.

I doubted Merlin would let herself be captured and said as much to the others. They conceded that her death was a likely outcome, but still hoped she could be brought to justice.

We'd see how things turned out.

My emotions were all over the place when I went to my parents' house that evening for a quiet dinner. Exhausted and soul-weary, I ate in silence. Fin ate with us, having been at the house, tending to Dove. After dinner, I went to see my sister. She'd always been fair-skinned, but her current pallor was just a little too close to that of a corpse for my liking. I brushed back some of her golden hair as I sat on the bed next to her.

"I'm so sorry, sister," I whispered. "I know I didn't get you into this. You wanted to come along to appeal to Silvermane." I sighed. "Though I guess I did get you into this, way back at the beginning of things with... Lord Hale and..." I couldn't speak, jaw clenched, infuriated. "He'll get what's coming to him I promise." I sighed again after that. I had hoped something I said would rouse her somehow. But she remained still. After a time, I lay down next to her and held her. "I'm here, sister. Take my strength if you need it. You need to survive." I couldn't live with myself if she died having protected me.

It was late when I left, even more fatigued. Fin and I returned to the inn where Silence and Ant were staying. I checked in on Ant, sleeping like a log, good. Silence wasn't in his room. I suspected I knew where he was and I was right. He lay curled up on the bed, waiting for me. He rose when I entered and wordless, came to me, holding me. My strength gave out and I cried into his shoulder.

He helped me into my nightdress and settled in bed with me, simply holding me, helping me to find the peace I needed to rest.

The next day was the same. More meetings and an evening with Dove, then crying myself to sleep in Silence's arms.

The sixth day after that fateful Noble's Council, we concluded our preparations and dispersed to arrange our various parts of the plan.

Dove remained unconscious, though some of her color had started to return. She'd live now, we all knew that, but the question became, would she ever wake?

I couldn't stay any longer. I had things to do, so I left her in the care of our parents and returned with Fin, Ant, Silence, Midnight, and the Fey to Cliffside. That night I spent curled up with Silence, Sparrow, and Ant, though we did nothing more than hold each other.

I wanted to go in now, face Merlin and get Alvere back, but I needed to wait for the others to move armies, which was never quick.

So I waited, day after day, growing ever more restless and distressed.

CHAPTER 22

ALVERE

WEAK AND BLOODY, ALVERE HUNG BY HIS WRISTS, WHICH were manacled above his head and now numb from lack of circulation. He wasn't sure if he wanted to feel them, given how bloody and torn-up they were after his various struggles to escape. The rest of his body wasn't much better. His legs ached, strained from standing on his toes to try to take as much pressure as he could off his wrists. These restraints weren't made for someone of his height. He'd made the mistake of using his Fey ability of manipulating cloth to escape. He'd almost made it. He would have, if Merlin hadn't been on her way to see him just as he'd picked the lock on his cell door with a stiffened strip of cloth. She'd taken all this clothes after that. Now he had nothing but the stinging lash marks Merlin liked to leave on him, and the bruises from when she brought Hale to rough him up. He was near to delirious with lack of sleep and lack of food. He got only a small portion of water and a moldy lump of bread every day, force-fed to him in no kind way by the jailer.

His keen ears picked up the soft padding of footfalls outside his cell. He knew those steps and had learned to dread them. Merlin was coming.

The key clanked in the lock and the door swung open, the light of the torch held by the jailer stung his eyes and he winced as Merlin strode in. At first, she'd come to him as a torturer, delighting in hurting him, healing him with her mists between sessions so she could continue her work. But now... she came as a seductress, in a wrap, made only of translucent mists.

She pressed her lips to his in a kiss which he didn't return. As she did, he felt more mists slip down his throat. He'd learned not to resist them, that only led to long, exceedingly painful choking sessions.

"You are mine," she whispered when she stepped back. "You might as well accept it, King Alvere. I've received word from the nobles of Vauphan. They don't care about you, don't want you back. *But*, they *would* be willing to take your heir to mold as their own. It solves all their problems, a new king without breaking the line of succession. And I, of course, would be a trusted advisor to the young king, being his mother and all." Her dark eyes gleamed with her lust for power. "So why don't you give me your child, a true heir of Vauphan for your people." She fondled his manhood, trying to bring it to arousal. He remained unstimulated, horrified by this woman and her insane plans.

"No," he croaked, voice dry and cracked. "I'd rather die."

She smiled but there was no mirth in it. "That is also an option." She raised a finger as mist formed a long blade at the end of it. She dragged that down over his cheek, biting deep, drawing blood. Then she ran it over his chest and stomach in a slow waving pattern.

And where she cut him, pain lanced into him, far more than such a cut should elicit. Her mists somehow amplified pain, shocking through him in throbbing agony.

He didn't know by what force of will he was able to resist screaming, but he did.

She leaned in and licked the blood off his cheek. "You can end this pain with pleasure. Give me an heir." She stepped back, and the gauzy mists around her vanished. "Am I not an attractive woman?" She reached down for his cock again, pulling hard on the limp flesh. "What will it take to get you to be with me?" She pressed her body to his, which only caused pain where she hadn't yet healed the long cut down his torso.

"Perhaps," she whispered. "If I looked like this?" Her form shimmered as mists covered her, then... in her place was Legs. She leaned in to kiss him again and this time, in a moment of weakness, delirious, Alvere returned the gesture, longing for his lost love, seeing her there with him. And now the stroking of her hand was indeed bringing him to the fullness of an erection.

"Yes, my king, I need you inside me," she begged, and though the voice was one he knew so well, it was then that he snapped back to reality.

"No!" he hissed again. "You're not her. You could never be her!"

The form shimmered and Merlin returned, growling in fury. "You are a stubborn man. You could have been free long ago, endured much less pain, if you'd only agreed to sleep with me. But no! You insist on pain! Well, then pain you shall have!"

With mist-claws on all five fingers of one hand, she

slashed it down over his body, gouging flesh, cutting deep. This time, he did scream, as she raked her claws over him again and again, lost to rage. Then, finally, she returned to herself, blinking, breathing hard.

She waved a hand and mists covered him to mend much, but not all, of his shredded torso.

"I am a benevolent host," she said, words belied by the insane fury in her eyes. "I'll give you one more chance. When I come next, if you don't pleasure me and give me your seed willingly, I'll just take it from you, then I'll make you suffer ten times what you just felt before I kill you. But, if you comply, you live. The choice is yours."

She released him and spun, leaving the cell.

Alvere was broken. He knew it now. For all his protests, he didn't want to die. He wanted to live to see Legs again. His will wavered. One moment he'd be strong, willing to hold out, hoping he'd be rescued, hoping he'd not have to face Merlin again. Yet, in the next moment his resolve wavered and he feared he'd submit to Merlin if she returned, especially if she disguised herself as Legs again. Would it be so bad to give her what she wanted, to end his pain with pleasure as she put it?

No! He couldn't allow himself to be weak. He had to hold on.

But his will kept failing him.

"Please, Legs, anyone, get me out of here," he whispered. It was his prayer; and he repeated it over and over until he had no more voice. Then he repeated it in his head. He didn't know what he'd do if Merlin returned before he was freed, and he hoped, he wouldn't have to find out.

CHAPTER 23

SPARROW

AS THE ARMIES OF THE ASSEMBLED NOBLES GATHERED TO THE north of the capital, those who would be going in, in secret, met on a farm that belonged to Maverick's sister, to the south.

It was a cool and rainy day with thick dark clouds over-head, which seemed to reflect the mood of those gathered in the barn.

Sparrow looked around at the grim faces of those who'd volunteered for this dangerous mission.

Legs, stalwart and brave, gave a curt smile as their gazes met.

Ant looked tired. He'd had a few days to recover after healing so many in Miraline, but still seemed fatigued.

Silence had turned hard, face set in a vicious glower. Sparrow didn't envy him his part in today's events, but he seemed ready for the gruesome task ahead of him.

Midnight was stoic and calm, as always.

Ahmaia, the Fey woman, stood a bit apart, ageless face unreadable.

"We may not be able to leave with the King," Legs said to Lady Ursa. The large woman wore armor which made her seem even more imposing than she already was. "If Merlin has cursed him the way she cursed the queen, we won't be able to take him too far from her, I'm guessing."

"Do we know any way to remove such a curse?" Ursa asked.

"Kill Merlin," Legs said bluntly. It was clear that was her preferred option.

Ursa grimaced. "I'd ask if there was any other way, but I think you're right."

Here, away from the Council of Nobles, it was becoming clear that capturing Merlin wasn't going to happen.

"A mistweaver is too erratic and too powerful to detain," Legs said. "The others of her House, perhaps, but Merlin..."

Ursa nodded sagely.

Spike, the leader of House Porcupine, spoke up. "There is no way to take her alive?" he asked. As the only other house leader here, he tried to be a voice of reason.

"Can *you* think of any way to disable a woman who can become mist at will and just float away?" Legs said, voice cool.

"Couldn't we knock her unconscious?" Spike asked.

"Have you ever tried that? It's a lot harder than you think," Ursa said.

"And how many people will die while we're attempting to beat her into submission?" Legs added. She shrugged. "Bring the manacles if you like and if a chance presents itself, by all means capture her, but I won't sacrifice any more lives if killing her ends this sooner."

Spike nodded. "Agreed."

We were set.

From outside the barn came the flapping of great leathery wings and the heavy thump of something large hitting the ground.

Everyone turned. Through the open barn doors, Sparrow gawked at the dragon-like figure. She'd never seen a Wyvern before. They were much larger than she'd thought. Standing on its powerful hind legs, it was probably the height of the barn, or so Sparrow assumed, only seeing the bottom half of it. The beast had no forelegs or arms, the wings took their place. Folding those massive leathery limbs back, it settled on the large knuckles at the joint of the wing. A long serpentine neck angled down to look into the barn. Thick scales — dark red with traces of gold — covered the being, a permanent armor over the massive form.

A moment later the form shrank to become Skyfire in battle armor, who marched into the barn.

"I'm coming with you," she said, her tone leaving no room for argument.

"As you wish," Ursa said, sounding dubious. "But at least let Lord Ant heal you. You look pained."

Sparrow had to agree. Skyfire looked rough. She'd lost most of her left arm and seemed to be favoring her left side. Sparrow hadn't been at the Council of Nobles, but she'd heard many versions of the fight, and in all of them Skyfire had not fared well.

Skyfire held up her remaining arm to stop Ant. "No. I am well enough to fight and the pain is mine to bear, a memory of my failure." She quirked a determined grin. "I may have lost an arm and a tit, but I still have one of each and that's enough." To demonstrate, she drew her sword and flourished it. "I wear my wounds with honor, as a memory of the day I couldn't protect those I loved."

The people she loved? From what Sparrow had heard, she'd been protecting Lady Silvermane.

"How is Lady Silvermane?" Ursa asked, as if Skyfire hadn't just admitted her love for another House leader.

"Still recovering. Her wound was grave, and she'll be on the mend for some time still. Healers are helping her regain... some... of what she lost." Skyfire's tone was grim.

It had become known that Silvermane had been pregnant when attacked. She'd lost the child. Sparrow could only guess at the torment the woman must be going through.

Sparrow leaned over to Silence. "Did you know Skyfire loved Silvermane?"

"Nope. That's news to me."

Sparrow nodded. At least she hadn't missed anything the others already knew.

"We're happy to have your battle expertise with us," Ursa said.

Skyfire grinned, a vicious and deadly thing. "You certainly will be." She passed Legs and nodded to her. "Drake tells me you're a House Leader in truth, now? Good." She slapped Legs' shoulder hard in camaraderie, nearly knocking Legs over. "Glad to have you." Then to the rest of the group she said, "Let's go kill a mistweaver."

"Our mission is to apprehend her, if possible," Spike said.

"Yeah, right, of course," Skyfire said, clearly ignoring the man.

Sparrow had to laugh at that, despite the dire times.

Legs turned to Sparrow. "You know what to do."

Sparrow veered into her bird form and flew out of the barn. The rain was light and the winds calm, so it was easy enough to fly to the capital. The first part of the plan was hers to undertake.

Sparrow landed in a dark alley and shifted back to herself, pulling up the hood of her cloak and stepping out into the street. It was quiet. A tense stillness hung over the city. By now, they'd know a large army waited to the north. Streets that should have been busy and bustling were empty. Those who were out, moved with haste, glancing about.

Sparrow turned a corner and headed for the Eel. The first thing she noted were the two large men standing outside in the rain. So, the Royals were being very careful. She approached and tried to simply walk up to the door, but a meaty arm reached out to block her way.

"Sorry, little miss," The one man said. "The Eel's closed to everyone but a private party."

Sparrow didn't doubt she could take both these men. They were hired goons, not Nobles, but subduing them wasn't the plan.

Instead she huddled into her cloak a little more and answered in a soft, scared voice.

"I'm here for Lord Jird."

"Another one?" one of the men said. "That old man's got some stamina. Wasn't there another girl here this morning?"

"Yeah, that's what you get when you're a Noble," the other man said. "Whores all day every day." Then he opened the door for her. Sparrow hurried in out of the rain.

Her gamble had worked. Lord Jird — a rather unsavory member of the Royal House — was a known lech, who lusted for particularly young women.

She tried to still her thundering heart as she approached the bar. There were other brutes inside the tavern as well, a full dozen tough-looking men. They weren't eating or drinking, clearly there to guard the place.

"Who're you now?" the barman said, suspicion thick in his voice. Several of the men in the room shifted, paying attention.

It didn't take much to make her voice soft and meek, a bit scared. "I'm sorry, good man. I... I was requested by Lord Jird. Told to wait for him in a room upstairs?"

The barman scoffed a laugh. "How old are you girl?"

"Seventeen," she lied. The one perk to being smaller and less developed than some other women was passing as younger.

"Twice in one day?" The man shook his head then shrugged. "Top of the stairs, third door on the left. Wait there and I'll let the good Lord know where you are when he comes through."

She nodded and left, slinking up the stairs.

She got to the room and closed the door behind her. That was the first part done. Now she had to wait for a while.

She opened the shutters of her window and lit a single candle, placing it on the sill. Luckily the rain was falling straight down and wouldn't put out the flame.

It was sometime later when a little brown mouse scurried in through the window. A moment later Silence was standing before her. She rose to embrace him, glad to see a friendly face.

"How'd it go?" he asked.

"Icky and nerve wracking, but no one suspected a thing."

He nodded. "My turn then." And he veered back into a mouse.

Sparrow's part was done for now. Others would arrive via this window shortly, but the next bit was all Silence.

CHAPTER 24

SILENCE

SILENCE SCURRIED DOWN THROUGH THE CRACKS AND CRANNIES of the tavern into the tunnels below. He'd been here before and knew the way well enough. Long ago, what seemed like a lifetime, when they'd been searching for Lord Hale after his attack on Legs, he and Foggy had scouted these tunnels extensively, but he'd never found the entrance into the Royal Estates. Now he was armed with the correct path through the warren of tunnels.

His mission was twofold. First to scout the tunnels and find out who or what might be guarding them. Second, to scout the estate itself and see if he could find Alvere.

The back room of the tavern had a trap door in the floor: the entrance to the tunnels, which was guarded by two large men. Neither were paying much attention, probably expecting people to actually open doors, which they'd notice. Silence easily slipped under the door to the room, and through one of the wider cracks in the floorboards down into the tunnel. He was just a bit surprised to find several more guards not far from the bottom of the ladder. They were down the tunnel a short distance, behind a barricade, facing the ladder. The make-shift fortification was mostly made of wood, with a bit of earth to help keep the planks in place. The men behind it would be mostly protected from anyone attacking from the ladder. And they had small slits through which they could fire their crossbows. Once on the other side of the barrier — no one paying much heed to the small mouse — he took a long moment to study the layout of the men and equipment. Of particular note was an area just behind the fortification where several thick, wooden poles propped up a wooden door in the ceiling. This hadn't been here before. Curious, he climbed one of the poles and slipped between the wooden boards above to see what he could. It was dim here, but sensing through his whiskers, he felt stones all around him. A chill swept through him. This was to block the tunnel. If people were coming down the ladder and it seemed like the forces down here wouldn't be able to kill them all, they'd retreat and pull down the wooden supports to drop these rocks down into the tunnel and block it. Which meant... Silence himself would have to deal with this, before people started coming down into the tunnels. But he'd wait for now. He'd do it on his way back from scouting.

He quickly navigated the maze of tunnels to the estate entrance. Here, two men guarded the ladder up. They were not on high alert, they would most likely be warned by hearing combat from the other end or from fleeing comrades. So, Silence snuck past them and up into the estate. He peaked up through the wooden floorboards just a bit to see the room beyond.

It was a stone room with a heavy metal door to one side. Two men manned this room as well, looking more alert than most of the other guards, but still bored.

There was another blocking mechanism in this room. What looked like a heavy metal plate, perhaps five feet to a side, and two inches thick. It was propped up against one wall by two planks. If those planks were removed and the plate knocked over, it would cover the trap-door and be very hard to move. So, these men would need to be dealt with before he left as well.

Now came the hard part... waiting. If it came to it and he was going to have to deal with the guards down here, he'd been told to wait — for as long as he could — to see if the guards switched at all. If at all possible, he'd want to eliminate the guards after a shift change, so that their deaths wouldn't be discovered quickly.

But he knew time was precious. It might mean the difference between Alvere being alive and dead. And that ate at him as he sat there, hoping and praying to all the Spirits that the guards would change soon.

He didn't know if it was seconds, minutes, or hours that he sat there, but finally, the door to the small room opened and men came in.

"Go grab some grub," one of the men coming in said.

Silence took the moment while the group was milling around in the room, to rush out from the trapdoor. He dodged boots as he scurried out the open door. From the size of the group in the hall, it was clear all of the guard stations here and below were being switched out.

Good.

Now he just had to find Alvere and get back here to deal with these guards as quickly as possible. He ran off to explore the lower levels of the estate.

It took some time, in this small form, to check the various doors and tunnels in this sub-basement. But then, finally he slid under one door into a dark room, letting his eyes adjust to the darkness from the barely-lit hall behind him. Mice didn't have particularly good sight, but he caught a familiar scent in this cell. He sniffed around until he was sure, then transformed back to himself.

"Alvere?" he whispered.

"Silence?" The voice was hoarse and so very desperate. It made Silence's heart break. Especially given what Silence knew was coming. "Are you here to free me?"

"No," Silence said, his heart shattering a bit more. "But!" he added quickly. "We are on our way. If I took you now, we'd not be able to get past all the guards." That wasn't entirely true. Silence was fairly confident he could deal with the guards and would have to on his way out, but the truth was they suspected Alvere had been cursed like the queen and couldn't leave without dying. But he didn't want to say that to the sorrowing man. So, as much as it tore at his heart, he lied. "I just needed to know where you were so we can come and rescue you. Don't worry Alvere, I'll be back soon with others."

"Silence? No, please, don't go, not yet." And Silence knew he couldn't. With no light in the room Silence felt his way around until he touched flesh. Alvere gasped, then wept. Silence's hand swept over naked skin, feeling the roughness of what he assumed was dried blood, and the raised flesh of long cuts. "Don't. Please!" Alvere begged, pain in his voice.

But Silence drew closer and raised his hand to find Alvere's face; it helped that they were roughly the same height.

"Don't worry, my love, we're coming, I'll be back soon." He kissed the man's forehead softly.

Alvere sobbed. "I... had hoped... so much..."

"And we're here. Can you wait just a little longer?"

More sniffs and sobs. "Yes, I can... but please hurry." The pure agony and desolation in the once-strong man's voice tore at Silence. He tensed his jaw.

"Yes, we will. I need to go now, to bring the others all the quicker."

"Yes, go," Alvere said, still weeping.

Silence, though it wounded his soul to do so, veered into his mouse form and ran from the cell, retracing his steps back to the room with the trap door. He pressed himself as flat as he could to squeeze under the well fitted metal door and before he entered the room, he glanced within. One guard stood, the other sat beside the trapdoor.

Silence had no desire to kill these men, but it had to be done. So, he hardened himself for what was to come. It was easy, knowing how his friend and lover had been treated. He cut out any sympathy for the guards and told himself they deserved what they got, that they'd kill him given half a chance.

There would be no mercy tonight.

He scurried out, between the legs of the man standing, then veered, returning to his normal form even as he drew forth a dagger and drove it up under the man's jaw, into his skull.

Without hesitation, he hurled a second knife, made for throwing, at the man sitting. The guard let out a clipped cry before the knife found his eye and sank into his brain. Then he was silent as he fell back, limp.

But he'd made a bit of noise...

Silence stood stock still, listening.

Had the men below heard that?

"Everything well up there?" One man from below shouted.

Bloody bones!

Silence whipped opened the trap door and dropped down, landing lightly to slash out quickly, again taking one of the guards before he knew what was happening. The other didn't have his sword out, but he tried to draw it. Silence was there before the sword cleared the scabbard, plunging his blade into the man's eye. The guard went down like a board, falling flat.

Like death coming quietly in the night, Silence stalked down the maze of passages to the five guards behind the barricade at the far end. They were all facing away from him. Two died before they knew he was there. The third fell before he could draw a weapon. The last two tried to fight him, but they had neither his training nor his cold rage and didn't take long to deal with. The fight made some noise, but not much. Silence was certain the guards in the tavern wouldn't have heard anything.

His job here done, he slipped back through the tavern as a mouse, past the guards in the back room back to Sparrow's room. It was quite crowded now.

He shifted back, grim and stoic. The others all gasped, eyes wide. He was covered in blood and must have looked quite the site.

"I know where Alvere is. They... haven't treated him well. We need to hurry."

Legs' face darkened, growing grim. She nodded, signaling out the window to those waiting outside, then they were off.

CHAPTER 25

I RUSHED DOWN THE STAIRS, BUT THE FORCE FROM OUTSIDE had beaten us to the common room. Dead men lay sprawled over the room and the barman was trembling in Ursa's iron grip. A gore covered Skyfire flicked the blood off her sword and grinned at me.

"I haven't had a good fight in a while," she said. It seemed losing an arm hadn't slowed her down much.

"This way," Silence said, still stone-faced and scary as The Blackest Pits, covered in blood and not even noticing. I had to run to catch up with him, even though I had the longer legs.

Silence kicked open the door to the back room.

The two men within lashed out at once, ready for a fight. My *Hero* gift rose, but Silence was done with them before I'd moved in. One man went down with his own sword in his gut, the other with Silence's dagger in his neck. Spirits, sometimes I forgot how quick he could be.

The rest of us hurried along behind Silence, following where he led us, past the scenes of carnage in the tunnels and up out the other side.

As we came up into the Owl House estate, Skyfire caught me by the arm. "The little man did all of that?" she whispered.

"He did."

"Amazing." She watched Silence stalking like death itself down the hall away from us. "You've got a good team."

"I do." We nodded to each other.

Skyfire and a small group would remain here, guarding our exit, while I led a second group to find Alvere. Once we'd returned with him and he was safe, then we'd all move into face Merlin.

I hurried to catch up to Silence. We found him stepping out of the jailer's office, keys in hand. I peered inside to see the jailer trembling but alive. Though, long shallow cuts had been traced over his torso, cutting open his shirt. The large, heavy-set man should have been able to crush Silence, but instead was a quivering mess.

Spirits!

This side of Silence was terrifying.

We paused as Silence reached a heavy metal door farther down the hall and unlocked it. As he did, he said: "Ant, he'll need you."

The large man, holding a lantern to shed light in these dark tunnels, nodded.

I steeled myself for what I might see on the other side.

Legs... Auwei was concerned. I knew she wanted to say more, wanted to console me before I even laid eyes upon my lover, but she had no words. Even with nine lifetimes of insight, there was nothing she could say in this situation.

Silence opened the door and we rushed in. Ant stepped to one side, shedding light on the scene and I stopped dead, sickened by what I saw. Alvere hung by his wrists. Blood — fresh and dried — covered his arms, dripping down from above. Cuts and bruises, old and new covered his naked body. He winced at the light, a limp and dejected form, hair sodden, his own waste around him. The stench of blood and worse hit me like a brick wall, but I forced myself forward to him.

Ant reached him first, laying a hand on the man to heal him as Silence unlocked his manacles. I caught Alvere as he fell, weak as a baby bird, his arms slammed down onto him, dead weight.

"Spirits of..." Ant breathed, and I saw the man's jaw go tense. "I never..."

"Legs," Alvere breathed looking up at me through hooded eyes, with heavy bags beneath them. "Is it you? I prayed." His voice was raspy and weak.

"Let's get back to the others," I said as we moved as a unit. I carried Alvere, but Ant stayed close, hands on the man, healing him even as we made our way out of the dungeons.

Once we'd reached the area the others had secured, I laid Alvere down on the floor, kissing his forehead, kneeling close as Ant continued his work. Sparrow had found a blanket and laid it over Alvere's naked form.

"He lost blood flow to his arms," Ant said, concerned. "They're... Spirits, I don't know if I can save them. The rest of the damage is mostly superficial, though his dehydration and exhaustion aren't things I can heal. He needs water."

"Here." Ahmaia was at my side a moment later, producing a heavy water-skin, seemingly from nowhere, probably from one of her many 'pockets.' She handed it over to Ant who dribbled some onto Alvere's cracked lips, wetting them. He licked the moisture away and Ant continued in the same fashion, giving him a bit at a time. The poor man drank heartily.

"Thank you," Alvere said, head lolling to one side, gazing at me. "I... knew you'd come. I wasn't going to give her what she wanted... I promise." He was still delirious, that was clear.

Ahmaia produced bread and slices of dried fruit. I fed my love slowly as he rested, helping him regain his strength.

"I'll stay with him," Ant said as those around us fidgeted, wishing to be away. We'd been here too long already, the chances of someone finding us grew with each passing moment. "He'll be safe and I can tend to him."

As much as I wanted Ant with me for the fight to come, I agreed that Alvere needed him more.

Remembering that he might be cursed and probably couldn't go far, I said, "Take him down into the tunnels and guard him there. Hopefully he'll be safe."

"I'll guard him with my life," Ant said.

Ahmaia used her cloth "arms" to lower Alvere down into the tunnels and Ant went down, continuing to tend to him.

Good. Alvere was safe and I could focus on the fight to come.

Time to face Merlin and make her pay for everyone she'd hurt.

We made our way up out of the basements of the estate to what we believed to be the main floor. Moving carefully, Ursa led us to the great hall.

Anyone we came upon was scooped into one of Ahmaia's pockets before they could raise an alarm.

We reached the closed double doors and I let my spider-sense do its thing, listening for any voices on the other side.

I caught a distant conversation.

"... matter of time before they send a force in against us. The city walls won't stop most of the Nobles out there. Legs in particular is a sneaky bitch!" This was Hales voice and I smiled at his compliment.

Yes I am, And we're already here, surprise!

"So, do your thing," Hale continued, "Look into the future, tell us how we get out of this!"

"I already told you, I can't!" Merlin shouted. Her voice consumed with rage and madness. "I can't see my own future. I saw only that legs would thwart the war and bits of that damned Council of Nobles, nothing after that!"

Now that was interesting to learn, and a Spirits-sent bit of good news.

"Perhaps you should try," Hale snarled.

"Perhaps you should die!" Merlin raged and I heard a heavy grunt, then what sounded like a body hitting the floor and sliding... for a while.

"Darling!" I heard Swan's panicked voice and running footfalls.

So... Hale was down?

I didn't think we'd have a better opportunity than this.

"Now!" I hissed softly, then veered into my spider to slip under the door.

A moment later, Silence, as a mouse, followed beside me.

I instantly got a sense for the large room. We were in luck, other than Swan and Hale, Merlin was alone, no guards. Hale seemed injured but alive, groaning as he struggled to sit up. I knew Swan wouldn't be an issue. The only remaining threat was Merlin.

I sensed Silence's soft padding feet as he scurried behind a pillar. I followed and once he was out of sight, he shifted back to human and whispered, "I told the others outside to wait till they heard the sound of combat, then rush in. I'm going to distract her. You stay hidden and wait for your time to strike." The smile he gave was half-crazed, half cock sure. "Don't transform and try to talk me out of it. I know what I'm doing. You saved me from the last mist-weaver, I'm not afraid anymore. I trust you to kill her before she kills me."

Wow.

The look in his eyes told me I'd not be able to talk him out of this wild plan. I just hoped I could hold up my end of the bargain. I bobbed my entire spider form in a sort-of nod.

Silence smiled, then veered back to a mouse.

We kept to the edges of the hall. Silence broke off at one point, but must have waited to act, allowing me time to get closer to Merlin, behind her.

I was almost in position when Hale hissed. "An avatar! Merlin, watchout!"

Across the room I saw Silence revert back to himself, but he was still some distance from Merlin. Hale must have used his ability to transform Silence back before he was prepared.

"Pits," Silence hissed.

"You!" Merlin called, then instantly she seemed to catch onto our plan. "Legs is here!"

Well, so much for surprise.

Silence let out a terrible, feral roar and charged at Merlin.

CHAPTER 26

Silence leaped at Merlin.

Not wanting to waist his distraction, I returned to myself and rushed in, swords drawn and ready.

Mist blasted out from Merlin. A tendril caught Silence's leg and smashed him to the floor so hard he bounced. I heard his grunt of pain, his bones breaking.

I couldn't help it, I shrieked in horror-filled rage as I stabbed at Merlin, but mists formed a solid wall behind her, stopping my blades.

The others threw open the doors and rushed in as Merlin turned toward me with an obscenely maniacal grin. "Did you see what I did to your little king?" she taunted me. "I'd heard he liked it rough, and yes, he did." Then she laughed.

A red haze of rage filtered over my vision.

She's goading you. She wants you to face her head on. If you do, you'll die! Auwei's warning stopped me. Furious, I jumped away as tendrils of mist reached for me.

I landed on the side of a pillar, then quickly bounced away, moving around the hall, trying to keep ahead of the mists lashing out at me. Finally, I threw myself over the railing into the second level balcony and out of Merlin's sight, hoping that would give me a moment to regroup.

"Come out little spider," Merlin called gleefully. She enjoyed this, playing with me.

"Continue to keep her busy, I'll get behind her." The voice was Midnight's and it was close. I looked around, but of course couldn't see her.

"Will do." I whispered.

It seems we're to be the distraction now, Auwei said. I heard the fear in her voice.

It makes sense, Merlin is already focused on us. Let's do this!

I whipped myself back out into the hall. As I sailed through the air, I caught sight of everything below me.

Merlin's mists had spread out, covering the floor of the hall. I couldn't see Silence and feared he was too hurt to get up.

Skyfire, moving faster than I could see, only a blur, dodged the mists grasping for her.

Ursa dragged Hale to one side. The man couldn't stand. Whatever Merlin had done had injured him greatly. Swan was nowhere to be seen.

Ahmaia flew on fluttering cloth wings, batting away Merlin's misty arms with cloth ones of her own, a stalemate for now.

Sparrow fluttered about in bird form, weaving through the tentacles of mist reaching for her. Spike was dragged down into the mists as I watched, his scream clipped off as he fell below the rolling waves of fog.

Merlin floated, raising herself on a pillar of mist in the center of the room, cackling, head thrown back, in a fit of ecstasy.

It only occurred to me then, that Merlin might be *more*

powerful than her sister, Hazra. If so... we were in for one Pits of a fight.

I landed on the side of another pillar.

"Over here!" I called, though I needn't have bothered, Merlin had already spotted me.

"Yes! Let's play," she giggled and with a wave of her hand, the mists on the floor spilled out farther around her. Skyfire tried to escape, but the mists caught her before she could use her incredible speed and sucked her down into their depths.

No!

Ursa wisely stayed back, but that put her out of the fight, too far away to do anything but watch. Ahmaia backed off as well, unable to get any closer with the mists rising to meet her.

It seemed it would be up to me.

And Midnight, wherever she was.

"Come on Legs, let's see what you've got. I'm slowly killing those I've trapped in the mists below, including that pretty young man. Let's see if you can save him before I kill him."

She was trying to split my focus, make me worry for Silence instead of concentrating on her. It almost worked. But I blocked out the trembling rage building within me — my *Hero* gift straining to be released — and closed my eyes to focus on my other senses. I could feel the billowing mists and the bodies trapped within it, Silence, Spike, and Skyfire, all twitching desperately. I also felt Merlin and her literal attachment to the mists. She wasn't floating on a cloud so much as her feet and legs had become mist. She was a part of all the mists in the room.

I didn't know how Midnight planned to sneak up on her,

but that wasn't for me to know. I was just the distraction. Time to be distracting.

"You want me, come get me," I shouted, then launched myself away, leaping around the great hall as Merlin lashed out with her mists.

"Oooh! You are quick aren't you! This is going to be so fun!" she cackled.

When I leaped next, she vanished in a puff of smoke and appeared in my path. Her hand moved and a larger hand of mist appeared to slap me out of the air. "Swat the little spider!" She giggled as I fell to the floor, hitting hard and rolling. I tried to leap away, but the swirling mists, as high as my waist, held me fast.

Pits!

"Is that all you have?" Merlin appeared next to me with a smug smile of superiority. Then her face contorted slipping through pain to rage. "How did you ever beat my sister?" she spat at me.

A fist of mist slammed into my stomach, doubling me over, and blasting out my breath. Without my armor, I was sure that hit would have crushed organs and scrambled my insides.

How *had* I defeated Hazra? I'd used all my tricks: my senses telling me where she'd materialize next, then I'd used my webbing to suffocate her.

I already had a hand on my stomach, doubled over from her hit. I spun out a ball of webbing into my palm. Then, as I righted myself, threw it at Merlin.

But she'd already puffed away to a spot closer to the middle of the room, laughing with glee. "That won't work on me. I saw how you defeated my sister. I know all your tricks. You can't defeat me!"

We'd see about that.

This time... I had help. My senses picked up the small flurry of movement as a sparrow landed on my back. I flashed into my spider form and Sparrow sped me away, high into the hall.

Only then, while I had the briefest of moments to take everything in, did I notice: the wooden railing at the edge of the balcony had a branch growing out of it.

Midnight could manipulate wood! That must be her.

Sparrow released me over the second level and I landed as myself, but didn't stay long, jumping away — in a different direction from Sparrow — on the move once again, keeping Merlin's attention.

I DESPERATELY EVADED HER SPIKES AND FISTS OF MIST, jumping around the hall in a frenzy, keeping Merlin's focus away from that branch. I just needed to keep her occupied a moment longer and...

Midnight appeared as she plunged down, knife in hand, but Merlin must have sensed something as she flinched at the last minute, the blade meant to sink into her neck tore down her back instead.

It didn't kill her, but by the screech of pain she let out, it had hurt like The Pits!

The mists in the hall suddenly contracted back into Merlin. Perhaps it was some defense mechanism? I didn't know, but I was thankful for it. Skyfire and Spike gasped for air. Silence, however, was a little too still.

I needed to help him.

But I also needed to help Midnight defeat Merlin.

My hesitation didn't help either of them.

Midnight cried out as Merlin caught her in a fist of mist,

then slammed her into a wall. Merlin screamed with rage crushing Midnight, who'd die if I didn't help now!

I launched myself at Merlin, just as Skyfire — as a wyvern — also chose that moment to attack.

Neither of us hit the madwoman.

CHAPTER 27

MERLIN SHRIEKED AN UNENDING SCREAM AS SHE SPUN, flinging out her hand. A circular blade of mist expanded out from her. It caught Skyfire and me mid-leap. Skyfire managed to get mostly out of the way with a flap of her large wings. I shot silk at the ceiling and tried to pull myself up as well. I pulled up one leg in time, but the mist-blade caught my other ankle. If not for my armored boots, it would have severed my foot, but still the cut was deep and bled profusely.

My *Hero* gift kicked in hard, blocking the pain even as I paused on the domed ceiling to pull more silk and clot the wound. It would be hard to walk or leap or do much of anything with that one lame foot.

Skyfire breathed fire at Merlin, who blocked with a wall of mist.

I had no clue how to stop Midnight from being crushed. Though... Merlin held out one hand toward Midnight as if controlling the mist upon the woman. So, I shot silk at her hand and tagged it. Then I yanked the silk and managed to pull the hand away. Midnight cried out and fell to the floor as Merlin's mists vanished, but it was clear Midnight had taken extreme damage and wouldn't be participating anymore in this fight.

"I've done what I can," she gasped. "Kill that bitch!"

I would be more than happy to oblige, but... how?

Merlin, with her arm now roughly extended in my direction, opened her palm and a wall of mist rushed at me. I leaped off the ceiling, though with my lame foot, it was more of an awkward fall. The mist-wall caught my shoulder, sending me somersaulting through the air. An uncontrolled fall from this height was going to hurt, a lot.

I braced myself.

Then Skyfire swooped in to pluck me out of the air. She too had a wounded leg. I guessed her tough hide had protected her from that attack the same way my armor had. Still the wound was deep and she'd quickly lose a lot of blood from it. I reached down and put some silk over it to help her.

An idea was forming in my mind. I'd gotten my silk on Merlin once. Perhaps, if I did it again, I could pull her to me, get in close where I could finally attack her. Skyfire and I were physically stronger than Merlin, so perhaps if we could get in close...?

But I doubted she'd let me get a solid strand of silk on her again.

And before I could act, Skyfire didn't quite dodge a slam of mist and we both went tumbling to the floor. I hit so hard, the bones in my right arm shattered on impact. Neither my armor nor *Hero* gift could prevent it. I rolled like a ragdoll and came to a stop abruptly when I hit a pillar.

All I could do was lay there and groan, even as my gift surged to reduce my pain. I got up slowly, it felt like forever. I couldn't quite clear my head and get back into the fight. A part of me wondered why Merling hadn't crushed me.

But when I finally looked up, I saw why.

Merlin — still floating, and seemingly fully recovered from Midnight's attack earlier — had captured Skyfire, who'd returned to her human form. Mists formed a noose around Skyfire's neck, lifting her as she flailed and gasped for air. Merlin cackled with glee as she turned toward me.

"You can watch her die, knowing you're next," Merlin said holding the other woman out in front of her, turning Skyfire to face me, so I could watch her die. Then Merlin formed a blade of mist extending out from her free hand and slashed it toward Skyfire's mid-section.

I screamed reaching out with my good hand, but could do nothing. The blade flashed in...

...but stopped, trembling, cutting no more than an inch into Skyfire's side. Merlin screeched with rage, eyes wide.

I didn't know what had happened and frantically looked around for an explanation. I saw Ahmaia. She stood next to Silence, who was now tightly bandaged in ribbons of her cloth. I hoped that meant the man was still alive. Ahmaia had her hand out toward Merlin, but hadn't used any of her cloth strips to reach the woman, so how...?

It was a testament to how dazed I must have been from that last attack, that it took me this long to figure out... Merlin was wearing clothes and Ahmaia was controlling that cloth, keeping Merlin from moving, even slowly pulling the mist-blade away from Skyfire.

Merlin's mists tossed Skyfire to one side. The woman hit the floor hard, gasping desperately for air and out of commission for the moment.

Even though Merlin couldn't move, the mists rotated her to see her attacker. Her shrill screech hit a new maddening pitch seeing Ahmaia. Mists lashed out at the Fey woman, who parried with the cloth "arms" floating around her, even as Merlin was pulled down to the floor.

"We have her trapped for a moment, what should we do?" I flinched, surprised at the voice next to me, but it was only Sparrow. "You well enough to fight?"

"I'm hurt pretty bad," I admitted, even if my gift was blocking most of the pain.

As for what to do. My plan to get in close to Merlin was the only one I had, even with a wounded foot and a broken arm. "I just need to get close to her. Can you distract her for a moment?"

"Me?" Sparrow whispered, terrified.

I smiled at her. "You're quick and agile. I know you'll be fine. I need you Sparrow. Spirits, we all need you!"

The fear in her eyes turned to a hard determination. "Then I'll do what I can."

She veered into her bird form, but even as she flew toward Merlin, mists were tearing away Merlin's clothes so Ahmaia wouldn't have control over her. Sparrow did a quick pass at Merlin's head, pecking with her small beak and the madwoman flailed at the attack with one freed arm but missed.

I had to act fast. My *Hero* gift ebbed, strained by the extent of my injuries, but all I needed was one good punch on Merlin.

Ahmaia had moved in, trying to capture Merlin with tendrils of her own robe. Merlin deflected the cloth arms with her mists. Sparrow flitted about with speed and grace, weaving to avoid the strands of mist trying to capture her. Another peck at Merlin's head and the mistweaver roared in rage. A large box of mist appeared around Sparrow, then quickly crushed in.

"No!" I cried out.

Merlin spun to face me.

But that gave Ahmaia the opening she needed to grasp Merlin with her tendrils of cloth.

"Now!" the Fey woman screamed.

I launched myself off my one good foot and slammed my fist into Merlin's face. The mistweaver reeled back, even as I kneed her in the stomach.

A bubble of mist — some instinctual defense — pushed myself and Ahmaia away, freeing Merlin.

But... I'd landed a single strand of silk on her face when I'd punched her. I pulled myself back in before Merlin fully recovered.

I grasped her neck and pulled her close. "This ends now!" I whispered, then pressed my lips to hers. She jerked and I could sense her trying to summon her mists, but my toxin had already affected her. She went stiff, paralyzed.

I slammed her to the ground, straddling her, and spun webbing over her mouth. Her eyes went wide with fear and rage.

A sword skittered over the floor to me. I looked up to see it had been pushed my way by Ahmaia of all people. The message was clear: even the Fey — who revered life — wanted the mistweaver to die.

I plucked up the sword in my good hand. "For all your crimes against Elista and Vauphan, for all those you've killed, for all the pain and suffering you've caused, I Legs, Head of Spider House and High Noble of the Realm sentence you to death." I slammed the blade down into Merlin's heart so hard the sword shattered when it hit the floor on the other side of her. I took the jagged bit still attached to the hilt and ran it across the woman's throat, for good measure.

Merlin twitched once, then stilled, vacant eyes staring at me: dead.

I collapsed off Merlin, the fight going out of me. Ahmaia caught me in tendrils of cloth before I hit the floor and lowered me to the stones.

I could hear the distant groans and whimpers of the others in the hall.

"Get Ant," I whispered to Ahmaia before I passed out.

CHAPTER 28

I WOKE, DAYS LATER, STILL IN A LOT OF PAIN AND SLIGHTLY feverish. My body was slowly healing itself, which begged the question: why hadn't Ant healed me? So many questions raced through my delirium-addled mind. I needed to know if the others had survived.

Auwei?

Yes, I'm here, but I don't know much. I've only been peripherally aware of what's been going on. Ant never came to see you. I don't know why.

Startled by my pained groan as I tried to sit up — and failed — Princess, who'd been laying on my bed in cat form rose and shifted to human.

"You're awake? Good. We were worried for a while there."

"Ant..." I said, barely able to form words, struggling to remain awake.

"Ah... well... about that. He can't help you, not anymore."

What?

Princess then gave the full report on what had happened after the fight.

The good news was, everyone had survived, but it had come at a cost. Apparently, Sparrow, Midnight, and Silence had all been so badly hurt that Ant had had to pull them back from the brink of death... but he'd nearly killed himself, burning out his spirit-gift, doing it. He could no longer heal. Luckily, he'd already healed Alvere before that, and none of the others had needed too much mending... except for me and Skyfire.

Skyfire had stubbornly refused healing. She wished to keep the scar around her neck and her now raspy, damaged voice as another reminder of her failure.

And even despite Ant's monumental effort, the other three still needed time to recover fully. So that's what we did: rest and mend.

Knowing everyone was alive, I let myself succumb to sleep once more.

It was about two weeks later when I woke finally feeling healthy and rested, my *Hero* gift having healed me far faster than normal.

Sunlight flooded the room, making me smile, even if it hurt my eyes a little. I blinked, pulling myself up to a sitting position.

It was then I noticed Lady Crane sitting quietly on a chair pulled up next to the bed.

"Good morning, Lady Legs," Crane said with a respectful tilt of her head. "I thought you'd want to know, your sister is awake. We got the news by pigeon late yesterday."

I smiled, breathing a heavy sigh of relief. I hadn't known how much that had been weighing on me until now. "Is she well?"

Crane nodded. "From the report, she is doing quite well,

and will soon be on her way here to see you and Lady Silvermane."

"That's a relief, thank you." I smiled, feeling refreshed by this news and the sunny day. I wanted to get up and move around. But before I could slip out of the large bed Crane spoke again. "There is more news... of a mixed nature." Her tone was odd, and when I turned to her, I couldn't read her expression.

She continued, "Lord Hale's trial concluded two days ago. He was sentenced to hard labor in the quarries of the north-west."

"Oh?" I'd really hoped I'd get the chance to face him, maybe kick him in the balls as part of his punishment. He certainly deserved it, but... I supposed hard labor wasn't *too* bad.

Crane grimaced. "But there was an attempt to free him. Lady Swan, who'd fled the capital after Merlin died, hired a group of mercenaries to attack the caravan." Crane tilted her head to one side. "I suppose I shouldn't call her Lady Swan anymore. Her title has been stripped from her, so I suppose she's just Swan now."

"An attempt?" I didn't like where this was going.

"Yes, the fighting was fierce and the mercenaries killed, but Hale was freed. He fled but was pursued by one of the Nobles escorting him... Lord Horn."

"They let his father escort him?" I blurted. I was certain Hale had escaped now.

"Indeed, and..." Crane sighed heavily. "Lord Horn was forced to kill his son to keep him from escaping."

I stared at Crane, wide-eyed. "Truly?"

"Yes. Hale is dead, and Lord Horn has gone into seclusion." She grimaced. "Swan escaped again, however. The search for her continues."

Wow. That was... mixed news indeed. I didn't fear Swan. She would be a pest at most, and probably soon captured as well. But the loss of Lord Horn... "That must have affected Lady Silvermane deeply."

"Indeed. She has stepped down as head of her House. As to who will replace her, that is still in question. Some in the House would like Lady Dove to take the leadership. But that will be decided internally."

Dove? That could be fun? Us two sisters as House Leaders.

I finally slipped from the bed and went to my wardrobe. Not caring if Crane saw me naked, I removed my night-dress and began dressing.

"Going somewhere?" she asked. Her tone suggested I should still be resting.

"I've been in that bed for how long?"

"Almost two weeks."

"Exactly. I'm fully healed now and I need to get out and see the world, see people."

Crane laughed. "You're more like Maverick than you know, young one. He never could stay still for long. Would you like an escort?"

I smiled at being compared to Maverick. I was a bit surprised the mention of his name didn't fill me with melancholy. Perhaps now that those behind his death had finally been brought to justice, I could remember him with peace in my heart.

"No, thank you Lady Crane. But... is Lady Skyfire up?"

"Yes," Crane said with a hint of disapproval. "She, like you, can't remain in bed for long. She's been up for a couple days now, despite her injuries." Crane huffed. "I don't understand her insistence on remaining injured."

I pulled on a loose white blouse. "Have you ever been in

such a pitched fight?" I asked Crane. I honestly didn't know. She usually stayed away from the fighting.

"I... have been in a few skirmishes in my time, but... probably nothing like what you or she went through, no."

I nodded. "We all carry scars from those fights, Lady Crane. Even if you can't see them, they're there, marks in your soul you have to live with the rest of your life." I gave a heavy sigh, feeling my own internal scars. "Perhaps, for Skyfire, wearing her wounds on the outside is a way to cleanse her soul of the marks on the inside." I looked up at Crane and smiled softly. "Or maybe she's just a stubborn and highly-irrational woman. I don't really know."

Crane laughed. "Did you want me to deliver a message to her for you?"

I nodded. "Yes, if you will. I'd like to have lunch with her."

"I'm sure that can be arranged." Crane rose and, to my surprise, stepped in to embrace me.

"What's this for?" I asked softly, returning the gesture.

"For everything you've done and I'm sure will continue to do for all of us, for our House and this nation of ours." She chuckled softly. "And for staying alive so I wouldn't be forced to lead this House." She squeezed me just a little tighter. "The shoes I'd have to fill would be far too large for me."

I found a tear on my cheek at her praise and kind words. I held her tightly too. "Thank you."

She was back to her usual dignified self when she released me. She walked with me from my room into the hall, explaining that we'd all been put up in Wyvern House's estate in the capital, Skyfire wouldn't have had it any other way. The others were in nearby rooms and Crane pointed out who was where before bidding me good day and going to deliver my message to Lady Skyfire.

I stood in the hall for a moment, deciding who I'd visit first. I knocked then entered the next room, not waiting for anyone to tell me to come in.

I interrupted Ahmaia speaking softly to Alvere. She rose sharply and nodded at me. "Lady Legs."

Alvere sat up in bed, looking far better than he had in the dungeons. I smiled at him, and he returned the gesture. "I'm sorry to interrupt, I can come back."

"No, stay," Ahmaia said, and I caught her glance moving between me and Alvere. "I've had many days to speak to my... my son. It feels so odd to say that." She smiled and her face seemed to light up with it. "I'll stretch my legs and let you two catch up." With another nod of her head, she began to make her way out.

"Thank you, ah... do the Fey have titles or should I just call you Ahmaia?"

She paused next to me, laying a pale hand on my arm. "You could call me Mother, if you like?" Her words were light, her meaning heavy. She seemed to see how that hit me and chuckled softly. "Or Ona, if that is more... comfortable."

"Ona Ahmaia? What does that mean?"

"For the Fey, any woman who is related to you, but not a mother, or sister, or daughter, is Ona."

"Oh... so not a political title, then?"

"We have been blessed to have little politics among the Fey."

I chuckled. "Yeah, that would be a blessing." I nodded to her. "Ona Ahmaia."

She nodded and left.

Once I heard the door shut, I looked at Alvere and mouthed the word *mother?*

He smiled. "I think that just means she likes you." His smile faded. "I've been trying to explain to her how I'd have to marry for my kingdom, not for love." His smile returned quickly. "But I think she'll always see you as my wife, no matter who I marry."

I sat on the bed next to him, putting my arms around him. He did the same as we leaned on each other. "I will always love you, no matter who you're with," I said softly but firmly. "I don't think I can give you up."

"I can't give you up either. Whoever I marry will have to learn to live with you."

That was the best news I'd heard all day.

When he lifted his head from my shoulder and turned to me, I kissed him softly. That led to a very long time of kissing and caressing.

He pulled back and we paused in our enjoyment of each other. "How are *you* feeling?" he asked softly. "I... I've only heard what happened, but some of what I heard..." he trailed off. He looked down and withdrew his hand from where it had crept under my blouse, becoming somber. "I'm glad you killed her." His voice was hard.

I pulled him close and held him for a long moment as his temper turned to tears and he wept. "I felt so helpless!" he sobbed. "And... I... I began to doubt you'd come. I didn't want to, but... it felt like I'd been there for ages, in the dark."

"I'm here now," I said. "And I'll never let you go again, if that's what you want."

He gave a sobbing laugh. "That might make it hard for me to be king."

"I'm sure your people wouldn't mind me sitting on your lap, holding you, while you held court and met with foreign nobles."

He nearly choked on his laughter and tears. "That would

be a sight." He drew in a long breath and pulled back. "But... I'll need to stand on my own, Legs." He sniffed a laugh. I joined him. Sometimes my name was just a bit... confusing. He tried again. "I'll need to stand on my own legs... Legs. And I'll never give you up."

I didn't know how it was going to work between us, but I was very happy he'd said that. I added, "With Fin around, I'll never be that far away."

He nodded.

Something in his beryl-blue eyes shifted then, his expression intense and heated. "Take off your clothes, before I tear them off," he said suddenly impassioned.

I did, and he pleasured me repeatedly as our desire spilled over after so long apart.

As such I was a little giddy when I slipped into the next room, which belonged to Sparrow.

From what I'd heard, that last attack from Merlin, crushing her avatar, had nearly killed Sparrow. Ant had brought her back from the brink of death, but not been able to mend all her shattered bones. She was still on the mend, wrapped in heavy bandages.

She smiled when she saw me.

"How are you?" she asked, as if I were the one still in casts and slings.

"I'm doing well enough. How are you?" I moved around the bed, standing next to it. She sat propped up by many pillows and I reached out to stroke her soft, brown hair.

Despite the pain she must have been feeling she smiled, a bright and cheery thing. "I'm doing a lot better now that you're here." The smile faded a little. "There's still a lot of pain and it's hard to sleep. A healer, one with a spirit-gift, but not as strong as Ant's, took a look at my left foot. She said it may never heal properly. She did what she could, but..." Her smile returned and she shrugged. "We'll see."

I couldn't understand how she was so lighthearted about all this.

"I'm so sorry I... I asked you to..." I couldn't quite finish.

Oddly Sparrow only smiled broader. "No, Legs, never apologize, not for that. My body may be broken, but my spirit has never felt better."

I cocked my head to one side, curious what she meant by that, as I came to sit on the side of the bed next to her.

She reached out to me with one arm — only a few bandages on it — and I took her hand in both of mine. "Legs, I... I was always so terrified to fight, terrified of... of being hurt... like this." I opened my mouth for another apology, but she went on quickly. "And when you asked me to help you, I was so afraid." Her smile seemed to brighten even more. "But I did it, Legs. I fought against a mistweaver. I distracted her long enough for you and Ahmaia to finish her. *I* did that!"

"And it—"

"And it was *glorious*," she said, cutting me off. "I've never felt so alive and brave and... and..." She sighed, her smile fading only a little. "And now I know the pain is worth it."

I motioned to her bandaged body. "All of this... was worth it?" I couldn't help but ask.

"Yes, Legs. Don't you see? I lived!" Her mood darkened just a little. "True, I only lived because Ant was around and he can't heal anymore, but still... I lived." Her green-eyed gaze met mine. "Yes, I'm in pain, but most of this will heal. I may limp, or ache a little on stormy days, but that doesn't matter." She beamed once again. "Now I understand what you and the others feel, what you go through, when you throw yourselves into battle. You know you're doing it because it must be done, because the nation needs it, or your friends need it. And... I knew that before, in my head, but I never really understood it, never... felt it. I do now."

I was a bit dumbfounded. "So, you'll be throwing yourself into battle from now on?"

She quirked a grin. "Once I'm healed, if I'm needed, I guess I will."

I shook my head. "Most people in your place would feel the exact opposite, I'm sure."

"Well, yes, the pain is bad, but knowing that I'm in pain because I helped the ones I loved and saved my nation... that makes it worth it."

"You're a strange little bird."

"And you wouldn't have me any other way."

"No, I wouldn't." I leaned in and kissed her gently. "Thank you."

She beamed. "You're welcome."

I sighed. "Sorry I haven't been to see you until now."

"That's understandable. You were hurt. And Ant and Alvere come to see me regularly to check in, then Silence started coming as well. He... seems different."

"Oh?" I hadn't seen him since the fight. "How?"

"More serious."

Silence had never really been a jovial fellow, always a bit somber. "*More* serious?"

"Yes. I think you need to talk to him."

"I was on my way there next."

"Then go. I'll be waiting, return when you can."

I nodded, kissed her again, squeezed her hand, then left.

In the next room I found Silence dressed all in black, standing with his back to me, gazing out the windows. He turned as I entered. Something about him, maybe the black suit, or how he stood with his arms clasped behind him, or his grim features, made him seem dangerous now, in a way he never had before. Certainly, the clothes looked exquisite on his slender form. Still, he smiled, if only slightly, when he saw me.

"Hello Legs."

I went to him, embraced him tightly. After a moment he held me too.

"I'm so glad you're alive and well!" I said into his shoulder.

I felt his head move next to mine, nodding. "As am I for you."

I released him after a long moment, standing back with my hands on his shoulders to peer into his face. "Sparrow said you were different, but this...?"

His smile appeared again, only for an instant. "Yes, dying will do that to you."

"Dying?" I furrowed my brow. "I heard Ant brought you back from the brink, but..."

Silence shook his head. "Perhaps that is the case, but that is not what I believe. I believe he reached into The Pits and pulled me from the grasp of death itself. I will forever be indebted to him. I believe it was bringing me back that burned him out." He shook his head. And with that one movement I understood the change which had come over him.

He wasn't more serious so much as in mourning. Mourning for his lost previous life, his youth, his innocence. Mourning for Ant's lost gift, which he believed to be his fault. He was a changed man indeed, and I had the feeling this sense of grief would linger with him.

"And what did you learn from death?" I asked. I wasn't sure where those words came from. They seemed to shock Silence as well.

"Learn?" He blinked. "Ah... well, I learned I didn't much like it and don't want to die any time soon."

I laughed a little at that. "And?"

"And..." He furrowed his brow in thought for a moment before he cocked his head to once side. "I learned that charging in against a foe with rage in your heart is a bad idea." He let out a self-deprecating laugh. "I honestly thought I could defeat her, myself alone, in that moment. I felt so powerful and purposeful and unstoppable. I thought I could get vengeance for what she'd done to Alvere." Silence grimaced, then shook his head. "But she... was so quick. Then I was choking on mists..."

I understood. I still shied away from the memories of when we'd found Alvere. They were too painful.

Silence let out a long sigh. "But now I know." Again, that fleeting smile surfaced and faded. "I'm not a front-line warrior, I'm... an assassin." He grew hard then, and I recalled the many guards he'd slaughtered in the tunnels. "I strike from the shadows, from... silence. I am cold, not hot with rage."

"I think you're hot," I said playfully.

The grin flashed again. Raising a hand to my cheek, he cupped it softly, and I leaned my face into his touch, closing my eyes. He drew me close, his lips to mine, soft and gentle. And despite what he had called himself, he was very hot with need soon after that.

What we shared then was a quick and impassioned love-making, a sating of hungers, not a tender moment. We didn't even fully undress.

"See," I said afterward, a little breathless. "You can still be hot and passionate."

"With you, yes, but not in battle."

I nodded, hoping I understood.

Crane found me in Silence's room. She knocked first and announced herself, so when she entered, it was to see us straightening our clothes.

She shook her head as she said: "Skyfire is ready for lunch in the atrium."

"I have no idea where that is."

"I'll take you there."

I kissed Silence good-bye. As I left, I looked back. Yes, he had changed. I'd never think of him as a boy again. He was a man now, and there was majesty in that, but also a touch of sadness.

CHAPTER 29

THE COUNCIL OF NOBLES LOOKED FAR DIFFERENT THAN IT HAD the day Maverick had chosen me for his house. So many of the faces I'd known were gone, and one entire house was missing. Owl House had been removed from the lists. Perhaps it would be replaced with another in time, but for now, its members who had not been involved with Merlin — which were few — had been given the choice of losing their title or joining another house. A few had come to Spider House, penitent and wishing for a second chance. I had granted them that chance.

I sat as House Leader, with Crane standing at my side. Others from my house sat in the gallery around us. Members of the public crammed into the theatre where the Noble's Tests were held. They wished to see who would be crowned king or queen, which House would be elevated to Royal.

Silvermane no longer wished to be queen. She'd stepped down as leader of her House and gone into seclusion. That meant we needed to select a new monarch... again.

Skyfire, now the most senior House Leader, rose to open the ceremony.

"Today we crown a new monarch for Elista!" Her voice didn't carry well, harsh and raspy, but she'd insisted on doing this, and not having Drake do it for her. "This is a solemn yet joyous occasion. And though our nation has been through turbulent times, I am certain that whoever is chosen here today will usher us into a time of prosperity and peace!"

She looked around at the others. I did so as well.

Next to Skyfire sat the next most senior House Head, Grizzly. Ursa stood proud next to him.

Lady Tanuki and her second Red were the next most senior. Then Lord Spike and his second, Lord Quill of Porcupine House.

I was now the fifth most senior House Head on the Council, since I'd technically been appointed to my post before Lady Margay.

Margay had disavowed the behavior of her predecessors and vowed that her House would be a strong supporter of peace with Vauphan. Her second was Lord Serval, a serious looking fellow, tall and lean.

House Pterolycus had been renamed to House Kitsune for its new leader. Lady Kitsune had been my instructor at Silverveil, and I knew she'd do well as leader of her house. She hadn't been involved in Fang's support of Merlin, but she'd still have a lot of work to do — like Lady Margay and House Panther — to prove herself in the eyes of the public and the Nobility... and she knew it. Her second was Lord Husky, a jovial man with a ready grin.

Finally, and a thrill for me to see, Dove was head of House Pegasus. She was resplendent in her silver Fey armor, looking every inch the leader. She smiled at me when our eyes met. It wasn't unheard of for siblings to be Heads of Houses, but it certainly wasn't common. Her second was her long-time friend, Lady Willow. Lord Horn had resigned his Noble status and lived in seclusion. Lady Silvermane had done the same. She now lived with Skyfire, wishing only for a quiet life, out of the public eye. I'd spoken to her briefly while staying at Skyfire's estate and she seemed a reduced version of herself. I hoped someday, with Skyfire's love, she'd once again be the strong woman I'd known.

All attention was on Skyfire, which she drank in with a grin. She would give her vote for the next monarch first. The rumor was, she'd vote for herself, which was allowed.

"I Skyfire, of House Wyvern, select my candidate for monarch..." She knew everyone was hanging on her next words and drew out her pause. "Lady Legs of House Spider."

I sat a little straighter. "What?" I whispered to no one in particular.

Actually, that doesn't surprise me. Auwei said confidently.

Oh?

Yes, she didn't want to be queen when we selected last time, why would that change now?

I thought she voted for Silvermane because she loved her. But me? Why me?

I think we're about to find out.

Skyfire went on. "Lady Legs was of pivotal importance in defeating the tyrant Merlin and leading the Houses in defense of our proud nation. I believe she would make a great queen for us all!"

Oh.

See.

No, I didn't, not yet.

Skyfire sat and Grizzly stood. "I second Skyfire's nomination of Lady Legs. When we few Houses gathered to move against Merlin, it was she who led us, who guided us. She, though young, has all the experience and wisdom needed to lead our nation into peace... and Spirits-Forfend it should happen again... into war."

And now I was starting to see. I'd seen it then as well, when I'd been called to meet with Grizzly, Tanuki, and Spike to decide how to move against Merlin. They were all life-long political Nobles and had little experience with what I'd been doing all of my — admittedly short — time as a Noble: fighting to defend my nation. They'd expected me to lead them and I had, with them as my Council. And that's when it clicked for me. I wouldn't be leading alone if chosen now. I'd have all of these Nobles to help me. I had little experience with politics, but they did. They could guide me through that, but it was clear to me now, as I looked around, that none of them wanted to lead. They were happy to follow... me.

Lady Tanuki voted for me as well, as did Spike.

It didn't feel right to vote for myself, so I voted instead for Lady Skyfire. She chuckled and shook her head. Clearly, she didn't want to be queen.

But other than myself it was unanimous. I was voted the next Queen of Elista. And when all the votes were in, everyone looked at me. The crowd cheered in the gallery and chanted "Queen Legs" and "Liberator of Elista!"

"Say something," Crane advised in a whisper. "Keep it short and simple, be gracious."

Thank the Spirits for Crane. I'd have her to help me as well.

I rose and drew in a long breath. Everyone hushed.

You can do this, Auwei said, sounding so very proud.

"My dear people," I said, raising my voice and hoping it

carried. "I thank you for your confidence in me. As has been said, I hope to bring only peace and prosperity to Elista. I am honored and humbled to be chosen as your queen and see it as my duty to serve you, the people of this great nation."

Another resounding cheer went up, and I sat slowly.

"Well done," Crane said, and I glanced over to see her smile of motherly pride.

When the cheering died down, a single voice rose above the rest. "Might I approach the esteemed Council of Nobles and Her Majesty, Queen Legs of Elista?" The crowd below parted, and there stood Alvere in full kingly regalia: crown, lush purple cape edged with pure ermine, and his usual blue-trimmed-with-gold suit.

"Approach, King Alvere of Vauphan," I said.

He grinned at me and stepped forward before the Council of Nobles. He took a long moment to look at everyone, then spoke. "Not long ago, I promised my hand in marriage to whom-so-ever you chose as your queen."

Oh! Right!

His gaze landed upon me. "I would like to keep that promise now, if it is the will of the Council and The Queen?" He approached, mounting steps onto the stage, then knelt before me. "Will you bring our nations together, Queen Legs of Elista?"

Pits yeah I would!

Please don't say that out loud, Auwei giggled.

I looked to the other Nobles. "What say you?" I asked them.

"This would bring peace and expand our influence," Lady Tanuki said evenly. Then, she surprised me by winking at me.

"Oh... just marry him, we all know you love him," Dove

said and everyone — after a moment of stunned silence — laughed.

I rose and went to Alvere. I gave him my hand and he kissed it, rising.

"Have you discussed this with the others?" I asked in a breath of a whisper.

"Yes, we've worked it out. Everyone's on board." He smiled.

Louder I said, "I accept your hand in marriage and bind our nations together in peace."

Another cheer rose up.

Alvere and I embraced in a sedate ceremonious way, exchanging a chaste kiss. And with that the ceremony ended...

... and so began the hard work of ruling not one, but two nations.

CHAPTER 30

THAT IS MY STORY.

If you're curious how I managed to keep everyone I loved close to me... well, it wasn't that hard. Lady Sparrow, once she'd recovered, became my lady in waiting, always at my side, so it was never awkward if she shared my suite of rooms. Silence and Ant became my — and Alvere's — permanent guards, so they were never far from our sides and were expected to be close to us when we retired for the evenings.

Silence eventually became the spy-master for our twin nations, and though he was often away, whenever he returned, he stayed with us. Luckily, being a master spy... very few people ever knew he was there.

Yet for all our secrecy, there were few who didn't know the truth of our little group relationship. In Elista, we were looked upon with joy, but in Vauphan, things were different. Alvere and I worked for a long time with the nobles to try to disband the hereditary inheritance of roles, but they fought us at every turn and didn't much like the uncertainty around the official heir to the throne.

My first child was Alvere's of course. She was born a little late, at mid-winter. Given the dark times, when we needed the light the most, we named her Dawn. She would not be an heir in Elista, but someday she might become a Noble and rise to the throne, if that was her destiny. Yet, she would be queen of Vauphan, no matter what. That much, at least, we were able to change. The Vauphani royal inheritance would go to the firstborn, not the first male child.

Dove married Fin and he joined her House. I was sad to see him go.

It was not always easy being the queen, especially during the war with Thraan. But that... is not my story to tell. That tale belongs to another, well... two others, actually. And when they are ready, I'm sure they will tell it, probably far more eloquently than I've told mine.

And so, I end my story, and wish you all the best in yours.

I remain your humble servant:

Queen Legs of Elista and Vauphan

Don't miss the next exciting series by Clara Wils!

DOUBLE DISCOVERY
Shadows Over Elista, Book One

All it takes is a single step to change your fate...

Asha may be young, but she's already faced many hardships in life. At twenty years old, she found true love... and lost it.

Uncertain if she will ever love again, she decides on a new purpose — one that doesn't involve a man in her life — and dedicates herself to her kingdom by bonding with a Lumani spirit.

She has no idea where such a union might take her, but bonding and going to Silverveil Academy is better than staying in a place where all her hopes for her future were shattered.

At Silverveil, she meets Dawn, a vibrant, rash, and reckless woman who's hiding her own heartache and searching for her purpose.

The daughter of royal parents who were busy ruling two nations, she doesn't know yet what her calling will be but knows it's not as a protected princess.

With guarded hearts, they dive into their studies and quickly make friends with a pair of confident, sexy twins, Tail and Agate, and the tender-hearted Boulder.

The men start cracking the walls around both of the women's hearts, but it's all just flirtatious fun. True love doesn't happen twice and it doesn't happen for a woman whose parents couldn't even love her... could it?

OTHER BOOKS BY CLARA WILS

THE GRECIAN GODDESS TRILOGY

written with Tessa Cole

Kiss of the Goddess, book 1

Power of the Goddess, book 2

Bonds of the Goddess, book 3

THE MISTS OF ELISTA

Bonds and Blood, book 1

Shape and Shadows, book 2

Form and Fury, book 3

SHADOWS OVER ELISTA

Double Discovery, book 1

Double Danger, book 2

Double Disaster, book 3

Double Doom, book 4

Double Destiny, book 5

SECRETS GODS KEEP

written with Tessa Cole

Craving Demons, book 1

Chaos Demons, book 2

Claiming Demons, book 3

www.ingramcontent.com/pod-product-compliance
Lightning Source LLC
Chambersburg PA
CBHW030141180626
46812CB00002B/792